PRAISE FOR *THE MARKSMAN: A KNIGHT'S TALE*

"When a global terrorist organization gets their hands on the mythical Excalibur with the intention of unleashing its unbridled power to conquer America, a military sniper known as 'the Marksman' answers the call to battle. This results in a confrontation between America's advanced super-weapons systems and evil forces wielding limitless supernatural power, interdimensional travel, and the strength of titans. The future of our world, and possibly the Multiverse itself, hangs in the balance. In this age of Hollywood superheroes and global terrorism, Dominic Pistritto has created a contemporary sci-fi tale that reminds us of the genius of Marvel's Stan Lee."

—John J Jessop, Author, *Murder By Road Trip, Pleasuria: Take as Directed, Guardian Angel: Unforgiven, Guardian Angel, Indoctrination*

"Reading the opening journal notes of an American contractor whose first name is Lincoln pulled me into this story. The adventure, fun, and mystique kept me reading and the drawings gave me insight. Even better, I really enjoyed the storytelling and look forward to the next book of this talented author. Congratulations to Dominic Pistritto."

—Mary Ellen Gavin, Gavin Literary Agency LLC

D1445558

The Marksman: a Knight's Tale

by Dominic Pistritto

© Copyright 2020 Dominic Pistritto

ISBN 978-1-64663-261-9

Illustrations by Rachel Vredenburg

Published by

3705 Shore Drive
Virginia Beach, VA 23455
800-435-4811
www.koehlerbooks.com

THE
MARKSMAN
A KNIGHT'S TALE

DOMINIC PISTRITTO

VIRGINIA BEACH
CAPE CHARLES

TABLE OF CONTENTS

This novel is dedicated to the life of Anne T. Pistritto
June 7, 1934 - Aug 8, 2018
"It's a good life."
We love and miss you, Grandma.

CHAPTER 1

Iraqi Desert, 0300 hours

THE SUN BAKES ME AS *I lie on the sand. Roland Industries has ordered a search-and-recover mission without air support. They don't want us to be seen. I call it suicide, but they call it efficiency. They want stealth under the most extreme and dire situations.*

I heard a rumor that a sword was the object of recovery, but I call bullshit. How could a sword have relevance in modern society? It's a barren wasteland filled to the brim with heat and death out here. My comrade Thomas is waiting, hiding under a bush not too far from my current location, so he's out of sight like me. I'm so afraid of failure. If this mission goes haywire, I may not live to see the end of it.

In all my years of critical missions and dealing with crazies, this one is the most mysterious. And this heat is making it hard to concentrate. I'm wiping sweat off this damn page. I hope this journal is found and read or even published one day if I don't survive.

Fighting off nerves is a battle I know all too well. The loss of my daughter left a serious mental scar, preventing me from ever having complete happiness. My wife would be devastated to see me like this,

God rest her soul, but I can't help it. The military tried their best to keep me out of combat, but I refused. They valued me too highly to watch me transfer to another unit even though I fought to make the change.

Those gunslingers think they can just take the lives of those they deem unworthy. I'm here as a reality check shot straight though their foreheads. I'm done watching those I care about most get hurt. I'm done watching people pay for the mistakes that the Souls of Death make every passing day, and I'm absolutely through watching idiots walk away unharmed from the problems that they cause. Those days are done. Until the next journal entry, if there is a next one, please remember me.

★ ★ ★

In the arid Middle Eastern summer, there was not a cloud in the sky. A man lay on his stomach, sweaty and hidden behind the corpses of withered, dead plants. His face was sandy and drenched. His legs had grown numb with both pain and sunburn. They were half-buried in sand from the stifling, malicious wind. His hands froze, cramped, as though they were about to give out. He was trained to endure such pain. He peered through the scope, waiting for that golden moment, the moment that would end the operation and years of terror for good. He lay in wait for the terrorist who had assisted in the 9/11 attack ten years ago.

"*Thaw, do you have a visual? Over,*" the voice in his earpiece asked.

Lincoln set his gun down and raised his other arm to tap the earpiece.

"Negative on that one, Thomas. Wherever this guy is, he's taking his sweet ass ti—" Thaw froze and squinted, suddenly spotting sandy clouds in the distance.

"I think I see him. Standby and watch my back."

"*Roger that,*" Thomas called through the earpiece. "*We'll keep you updated. You do the same.*"

Lincoln glared through the scope at the distant black Suburbans rolling through the desert. He watched for a few minutes until they stopped only a few hundred yards away. It was a decent distance for a shot. He watched as men in Arabian military-issue uniforms quickly got out of each vehicle. They wore the stern expressions of people who were responsible for a lifetime of deaths. Lincoln knew he had to make the shot before they could do any more damage. This mission was critical.

He watched through the scope as a few more men disembarked. Several wore white mesh sniper veils to protect their faces from the harsh sun and windswept sand. He grunted with disgust. He despised Arabian soldiers; they were responsible for the deaths of so many people, many of whom were among his closest friends.

He swiveled his head to wipe the sweat from his eyes, which distracted him momentarily from his target, Hakim Gorroff. He was first in command of the terrorist group referred to as the Souls of Death. He was middle-aged with wild gray hair. His organization believed that only their culture should survive after the second coming of Allah. They were initiating a mass genocide with Hakim at their command. They were succeeding in locations across the US, with explosions detonated at highly populated areas, including movie theaters, strip malls, and even neighborhoods of American citizens.

That was where Uncle Sam drew the line. The US began sending troops years ago, but they were inevitably slaughtered in battle. Lincoln couldn't stand the thought of family members living in horror, grieving the loss of their loved ones. One of his closest friends, Benjamin Frost, had been injured on the front lines. He had taken multiple grenade explosions and gunfire in heavy combat, decimating his squadron. Miraculously, he found cover behind a fallen helicopter as the barrage struck. He lay on the scorching hot sand for hours before his support team finally arrived. They expected more survivors when they located him. Ben was near death, writhing on the ground with his leg badly burned. Lincoln still cringed at the memory of his best friend sprawled out on the sand. The image fueled his hatred for the Souls of Death.

The men before him shook hands stoically. He tapped his earpiece and listened to the feedback from high-frequency microphones his team had placed around the site.

"I've come a long way to see it," said Hakim, turning to face the other men. *"The last men who lied to me are now six feet underground."*

"You won't be disappointed," said one of the other men. *"What we have here is valuable even to the Americans and Russians. It was smuggled away from the Nazis for its power. It's extremely rare."*

"You hearing this?" Thomas asked. *"What in God's name are they talking about?"*

Lincoln didn't respond. His eyes were fixed on the metal case a soldier pulled from the Suburban. The case had a large spherical bottom and a sharp top. He saw a digital lock on the side of the case.

Two men brought it to Hakim and set it down with a grunt. Hakim stepped forward.

"Open it," Hakim commanded.

Lincoln wrapped a finger around the trigger as the soldier bent down and tapped his fingers on the digital buttons to unlock the metal box. A hiss emerged from the sides of the box, and everyone stepped back in awe. A bright, golden glow emanated from inside. Hakim's eyes grew wide. The box was tilted in such a way that the inside of the case was visible.

"It's beautiful beyond compare," Hakim said, astonished. *"Where was it?"*

"It was buried in the mountains," a man responded.

"Why is the blade it still encased in rock?" Hakim asked.

"We couldn't risk damaging the weapon, so we opted to transport it and the rock to the base to safely remove the rest of it, sir."

Lincoln felt a wave of panic. Should he shoot now? Tell his team to retrieve it? His heart raced, but he remained fixed on the golden glow from the metal box.

The golden blade glistened in the sun and appeared to have been forged by the world's finest blacksmith. The hilt of the blade was also golden, surrounding the black leather handle where the wielder would hold it.

Lincoln scanned the landscape and spotted a few gas tanks behind the black SUVs. If he somehow managed to shoot the tanks, he might have a chance to ambush them while they were distracted. He quickly put his hand to his earpiece.

"On my mark, open fire and retrieve that thing. We have to bring it back to HQ. Do you copy, Thomas?" Lincoln's heart raced.

"Roger that. Squadrons one and two are on standby. Call it, Thaw."

Lincoln positioned the gun and angled the scope to get a better view. He could barely see the gas tanks through the window of one of the cars. He took a few breaths and counted to three.

"One," he whispered. He kept thinking about the beautiful artifact in range of his firearm that he was about to potentially destroy. "Two." He tightened his grip on the handle so hard he could feel his pulse. He closed his eyes, took one last breath, and thought of his old friend Ben lying helpless in the sand. He opened his eyes and allowed his rage to become his greatest ally. "Three." He squeezed the trigger.

BANG!

The bullet soared through the air and traveled straight through the car. Lincoln's heart dropped to his stomach. Every man whipped his head around, screaming and pointing. Lincoln inhaled slowly, targeting the gas tanks again and pulling the trigger once more. The bullet traveled even further. In a blink of an eye, half of the Arabians had been torched in a massive explosion. One of the Suburbans had gone up in flames, blazing into the atmosphere and raining death all around. Lincoln fired once more and ripped off the earpiece.

"Go, Thomas. Sections one and two engage!" He sprinted down the sandy incline, trying to keep from falling as adrenaline pulsed through his veins. He swung the rifle strap over his shoulder as he ran. He heard gunfire in the distance and saw the sand below kick up as the bullets pelted around him. Screams echoed everywhere as he dove to the ground. A helicopter soared overhead, strafing a shower of gunfire. Four men running toward him suddenly fell and lay motionless. He struggled to his feet and ran toward the artifact, expecting it to be destroyed or incinerated.

But to his amazement, the sword still sat wedged in the stone, completely untouched and glistening as if nothing had happened. He reached to touch it but froze when he felt an arm snake around his throat from behind. A remaining Souls of Death soldier suddenly grasped him in a choke hold and tugged him backward. Lincoln brought his foot to his chest to remove his boot-strapped stiletto knife. He plunged the blade into the man's arm and spun out of his grip in one swift motion. He retracted the blade and toppled back. The man fell to the ground, holding his arm. He clambered to his feet as blood streamed from the knife wound. Lincoln rose and stood in battle stance. The man removed a .22-caliber pistol from his holster and aimed it at Lincoln's head. He sighed.

"That's not fair," Lincoln groaned.

The man screamed and ran at him just as an ear-piercing shot ricocheted through the flesh of his head. His body slumped to the ground.

Lincoln turned to see Thomas in his trademark tan military uniform with the American flag patch emblazoned on his arm. He wore holstered firearms on each leg just in case. The brilliant sun reflected off his aviators.

"I had him, you know," Lincoln said.

"I know," Thomas said, sidestepping and walking past him. Thomas's platoon followed him to the strange artifact encased in the stone. It lay on the ground, glistening. Thomas's eyes widened as he marveled at the sight.

★ ★ ★

Lincoln was always the most precise individual Thomas had ever met. He'd started his career as a neurosurgeon at twenty-three, helping wounded soldiers during Operation Iraqi Freedom. He performed everything from brain surgeries to simple first aid. He had the steady hands of a surgeon, and he used that God-given talent to help everyone he could, including himself. However, his role in the medical field grew tedious, and he eventually became hungry for more action.

As his interest in his medical career waned, the government wanted him to remain an asset to the field medic team. But he refused: he wanted to use his keen precision and intellect for a higher, deadlier calling.

Lincoln began combat training and, after six months, had become one of the world's greatest snipers, second only to Chris Kyle. He could hit a soda bottle from a mile away, whether he was stationary or on the move. He hit his mark every time. He could leave someone as a vegetable, kill them, or leave them wounded. He was truly one of the most dangerous men in the US Army.

For his part, Thomas Lunardi was Thaw's best friend. They met in boot camp and instantly disliked each other. Lunardi was always one for competition and tried to make Lincoln look bad. However, to Lunardi's dismay, Thaw was training every day, even after curfew. Thomas soon realized there was no stopping Lincoln, and from then on, there was never hostility between them. Each knew one was always going to try to out-do the other. Lunardi was lucky that Lincoln had a sense of humor or else they would be in constant competition. They continued to be close allies on the field and always worked together to devise a plan with reasonable action to save lives and win in combat.

"We went through all this trouble for some stupid-ass sword," Thomas said. "Well, that was two months I'll never get back."

"If we came all the way out here for this, there's probably a damn good reason for it," Lincoln said. "Don't you remember when Gorroff mentioned the Nazi Party and the Cold War? Obviously, there was a reason for it. Someone get a bag. We're bringing this artifact home."

Lincoln bent down and saw the artwork emblazoned on the hilt. The pommel seemed to be crafted using some sort of serrated teeth bound together as if it was from the Viking era.

"This thing better have been worth it," Thomas said to Lincoln.

"You'd be surprised what a simple artifact like this is worth," one of the soldiers said. "But that doesn't explain why they would put it in a case locked away until now."

They finished securing it as a helicopter flew overhead. It landed two hundred yards away, sending up a hailstorm of sand. Thomas picked up the artifact and walked to the helicopter. He handed it to the man inside, and they immediately took off. Thomas turned around to face the platoon. "Let's move out," he said, and with that, everyone returned to their trucks.

★ ★ ★

The drive back was long and grueling. Water was scarce out here in this lifeless land of sand. The base was only a few miles out, and everyone was ready to get home and bring the package back for further investigation. Lincoln gazed out the window as they drove, pondering what Ben was doing back home.

He watched as the mountains of sand passed by the window. He reached into his pouch and pulled out a picture. It was of the three of them: Ben, Thomas, and himself. They all held fishing poles and tackle boxes as they stood next to a pier. It was a sunny day; the water looked calm in the background. Thomas held a large-mouth bass aloft with the hook still in its mouth. They all wore goofy expressions. It was the day they came home from the hospital after Ben was released. Ben's face was scarred and battered, but he still wore a smile in the photo.

Lincoln smiled and closed his eyes, remembering the excitement of that day, the tug of the line, and the fight from reeling in the huge bass. He opened his eyes and flipped the picture over. The date was written in black Sharpie: 6/12/07. A moment later, a voice snapped him back to reality.

"That bass was almost as big as Ben's ego," Thomas remarked. He slid over the bench seat in the back of the Rover to sit next to Lincoln.

"When we get back, we have to tell Ben about the sword," Lincoln said, sliding the picture back into his pouch. "He'll lose his mind when we show it to him. You know how he is with weapons."

"He likes guns, not swords. But I think he'll like it, nonetheless. Ya know, this may end up being classified."

"Maybe. But we still have no idea what or why we had to go through all this trouble for this thing. We should keep it and frame it in one of our living rooms. Maybe above the fireplace. What do you think?"

"Bullshit. I think it belongs in a museum," Thomas said, pulling out a cigarette. "I know I'd accidently scratch it or some shit."

"But what if some kid decided to reach over and touch the blade? What then?"

"They'd get kicked out of the museum," Thomas said, lighting his cigarette. He inhaled deeply and puffed out smoke. Lincoln shook his head.

"You know what they say about antiques?" Lincoln asked.

"No, what?"

"They hold a place in time." Lincoln rested his head on the window.

The team was happy to reach base, their home away from home. It was teeming with soldiers walking, running, and testing equipment. It was cloaked from above so the Souls of Death couldn't detect them through radar. The base itself appeared like a vast white utopia, with white pavement everywhere to reflect the harsh rays of the desert sunlight.

The base had been funded and built by a private enterprise called Roland Industries. They were the multi-billion-dollar corporation that created weapons and bases around the globe for all branches of the military. Roland Industries also specialized in funding teams dedicated to perfecting the biomechanics of prosthetic limbs of all kinds. They had contributed to incredible breakthroughs that increased the speed of healing in the epidermis. Roland Industries reached far and wide, creating jobs for millions and technology that would shape the future for years to come. Their slogan read: "Everything's Achievable through Knowledge and Perseverance."

One of their most well-known bases was located in Norfolk, Virginia. Charlie Roland considered numerous other destinations in the world, but he chose Norfolk due to the heavy overhauls of nuclear vessels there. In addition, the Defense Department maintained four public shipyards there that opened the door to many new jobs.

With so much at stake financially, it was only logical that they secretly withheld the money to create a bunker that stored thousands of failed prototype weaponry that never saw the light of day. Roland paid attention to that project for only three months before it was given to his assistant director, James Clinton.

The fence to the base opened, and the three trucks entered carrying the artifact. Guards stood at either side of the doors as the trucks rolled in with their engines roaring. Thomas watched as they rolled into the well-lit garage. They crept forward slowly until the truck came to a halt. Soldiers disembarked from the trucks in single file.

A door opened a moment later, and from it a man emerged wearing a brown suit and carrying a clipboard. He stood five foot nine, with a red tie, gelled hair, and a sly smirk. If looks could win him something, he'd get an Oscar. There was James Clinton, the Assistant Director of Roland Industries.

"How was your mission? Went well, I presume?" he asked, holding the clipboard behind his back.

Thomas approached him and smiled. "You're gonna love the hell outta this. Lincoln and I retrieved what you wanted."

"I hope so," Clinton responded. Thomas's slang was alien to Clinton. He considered his English superior to that of other people, so he sometimes struggled to decipher what exactly the cigarette-scented man said.

"Let's see it, then," Clinton retorted with curiosity.

Thomas and Lincoln watched as the other soldiers approached the truck and opened the doors. Two men grabbed hold of each side of the artifact and set it down with a thud. Clinton's eyes grew wide, and he turned to face Thomas and Lincoln.

"Keep in mind I blew this thing up, killing Gorroff in the process," Lincoln said as James stepped closer to it. James put out his hand and grabbed hold of the tarp, moved it over, and pulled it down. His eyes grew even wider as he gazed upon the golden blade. Thomas smiled as he watched Clinton staring at the exposed hilt.

"It's . . . beautiful," Clinton said, touching the side of the blade but quickly letting go. The metal was unusually hot. Given, it was in the middle of the desert, but this was a different type of heat. As if it were emanating from the blade itself. He imagined holding the sword near the cross guard and moving his hand near the hilt in astonishment. Snapping out of his dreamlike vision, he stood back up and looked at Thomas.

"Lunardi, I want a full mission report on my desk tomorrow morning," Clinton said. "And Thaw—" Lincoln whipped his head from the sword to acknowledge him. "I want this thing in the lab ASAP." Clinton turned and walked back through the door.

"He is such a hard-ass," Thomas said, shaking his head.

"Well, let's do what he said and get this thing to the lab," Lincoln said. "You've got some paperwork to do. We still have no clue why we risked our lives for that thing." He picked up his pace and ran through Clinton's door. Clinton was already halfway down the hallway when Lincoln caught up to him, clapping his hand on his shoulder.

"Still haven't answered our question. Why did we risk our lives?"

"Mr. Thaw, I seem to remember you were under orders to seek and recover an artifact for Roland Industries. Am I correct?"

"Correct," Lincoln muttered. He already knew Clinton wasn't going to answer him. *That dapper son of a bitch had secrets only God knew,* he thought.

"Then I would move on and focus on the next mission at hand. That sword is now classified and the legal property of the government. You're to forget it ever happened. Good day, sir." He turned and continued walking briskly down the long corridor.

Lincoln stared at the wall with his hands trembling in anger.

He turned and walked back to Thomas, who plucked the stub of his cigarette from his mouth and tossed it to the ground, crushing it with his foot in disgust.

★ ★ ★

Four hours later, the sword in the stone was analyzed around the clock in a mad frenzy to figure out what strange secret it held underneath its earthy surface. They returned no traces of hidden devices. A man in a white lab coat took notes and paced around it. Clinton walked up to the man.

"Anything?" he asked.

"We haven't found anything on the structure at all. The most we've found is the dirt on the blade."

"I'd like to see some kind of result. We're paying you to find answers, not questions," Clinton stated.

Clinton was always a complicated person, immersed in thought over an upcoming solution to a problem for the company. He was a mad thinker.

He worked his way up in Roland Industries until he found himself signing contracts for the company. Charlie Roland was the man who hired him, the president and founder of the worldwide company. Clinton always tried to prove himself worthy, regardless of what his boss thought. If Mr. Roland had a problem, he didn't have to worry, because James would solve it immediately. Clinton was the company's smartest person, a valuable asset.

However, he had a dark side as well. People had spread rumors secretly that someone killed his parents when he was younger, and he went insane in the aftermath. Someone thought that he went into black-market distributing. He could hurt someone physically and emotionally if he was backed into a corner.

CHAPTER 2

THE NEIGHBORHOOD WAS BRIGHT AND radiated with life. Green lawns, kids playing, neighbors washing their cars, and the sound of Lincoln's best friend Ben muttering every curse word imaginable as he tried to fix the muffler on his white 2008 Sedan Limousine. He was a driver for a limousine company named Luxury Wheels.

When Ben was discharged from the military, he needed a place to work to get some extra cash for his family. They hired him after two weeks, and he worked for the company for the past three years. The company even gave him one of their limos because he had done such a good job maintaining them.

There had been incidents in the limo, with clients trashing the car in different ways. That limo had been through thick and thin with him ever since he got the job.

The sound of a car rolling up on his driveway distracted him from his frustration with the muffler. He saw Lincoln and Thomas get out of their Land Rover and walk up his driveway.

Benjamin Frost was a tall, slim man with messy blond hair. He was a complicated individual. He loved spending time with friends and family, but every now and then, he loved to take a drive away from the craziness of day-to-day life. Survivor's guilt flooded him with agony when he got back to the States. Weeks turned into years of psychological and emotional therapy. He gradually got better but continued to struggle with the thought of being discharged from his squadron. His guilt was often overwhelmed with family responsibilities, running his business, and his friends who loved him.

"Still having problems with your limo?" Thomas asked.

Ben sighed and got up from beneath his car. His white T-shirt was grease-stained and tattered.

"What does it look like, buddy? I've been trying to fix this God-forsaken thing for months, and it's no closer to cooperating."

"Maybe it's about time you got a new one," Lincoln said. "Maybe a fancier, updated version. You always did talk about getting a new one."

"Because I want my ride to be the best it can be. These damn people that I drive around keep screwing it up, and I keep having to fix it. It's ridiculous, but it's almost done. But enough about me. How was the mission? I heard you guys found some sword in the stone or something like that?"

Lincoln and Thomas froze. They thought it was classified.

"You guys do remember I have connections, right?" Ben asked, laughing. When he was done with the military, he still had people feeding him intel. It was needed just in case anyone was to target him or anyone he loved.

"Well, yeah, we found a little sword in the stone," Lincoln said. "Clinton's having people examine it now."

"God, I don't miss that bastard," Ben said. "The amount of times I had to hold back punching him in the throat was unbelievable. How is he, anyway? Happy? Oh wait, I forgot, he doesn't even know emotion of any kind." He walked over to his refrigerator and grabbed a beer. He cracked it open and nodded to Thomas and Lincoln. They nodded back, and Ben pulled out two more cans.

"Well, he's still a stiff," Lincoln said. "I mean, it doesn't get better than that for him. Wouldn't it be weird if he was happy?"

"He's been doing all right," Thomas said. "He's more cutthroat than ever, thanks to this sword we found. We'd be celebrities by now if it turned out to be Excalibur."

"Don't even joke like that," Lincoln said. "It's bad enough as it is. We got Clinton up our asses about how we actually retrieved it."

"Either way, you guys managed to find an ancient relic that Roland Industries might use in the future," Ben said, swigging his beer. "Hopefully that'll be a good thing."

Each man knew of Charlie Roland. He'd done questionable things in the past to people who crossed him or pissed him off. At one point, he tried to wipe out the Coast Guard altogether because of his desire to fund high-powered submersibles that would eventually replace the entire Coast Guard fleet. The government deemed it too expensive for brand-new technology like that to be in their grasp so they never went through with it. Many people feared him because if he had just one idea, that usually meant somebody was at risk of either losing their job or losing their business as a whole.

"Well, if y'all wanna come in, be my guest," Ben said. "Veronica is cooking up some spaghetti and meatballs tonight. It's the kids' favorite." He walked to the garage door.

As Lincoln opened the door, he was bombarded with small arms hugging both his legs from two kids radiating with happiness.

"Hey, hey, hey! You guys get bigger every time I see you!" Lincoln said. He knelt down to hug the kids. Zachary was five and Theia was three. They always seemed to be smiling. Zachary was a small child in a black New York Islanders T-shirt. Theia wore a bright yellow dress that always swayed around whenever she spun in a circle. She always loved dresses, a trait she got from her mom. After hugging the kids, Lincoln stood and reached his arms out to hug Veronica. She did the same to Thomas as well.

She was a beautiful, tall, slender woman; she had short, jet-black hair and wore a Batgirl T-shirt and stared at them with dark green eyes. Her smile could make anyone feel better. Ben loved that about her. She had always been friends with the three of them but quickly grew closer to Ben. It wasn't long before they were married and had these two lovely kids.

"Zach, Theia, why don't you go play outside for a while?" Veronica suggested.

They scampered outside, almost toppling each other in the process. Once the door closed behind them, Thomas turned around and looked at Veronica.

"Why's Theia wearing a dress when she knows she's gonna get it ruined outside?" he asked. Veronica sighed.

"I can't get the thing off her. She's always saying it makes her feel like a princess. But you can't say no to them sometimes, am I right?"

Ben walked up and kissed her on the forehead.

"But enough about us," she said. "How are you guys? Haven't seen you in a long time."

"Well, you know, just pointing, shooting, and taking orders, you know?" Thomas said. Lincoln jabbed an elbow into his ribs, and Thomas let out a slight huff of air.

"What this idiot meant to say was that we've just been trying to make things work and make sure powerful weapons don't get in the wrong hands," Thomas said, rubbing his ribs.

"Yeah, that's been our biggest job lately," said Lincoln.

"I'll shoot you if you do that again," Thomas said.

"Please, nothing would thrill me more," Lincoln said. Ben and Veronica laughed.

"Yeah, I kind of miss being on the force with you guys," Ben said. "But I can't live that life anymore with the kids. I don't want to constantly leave them behind." He had been a different person before meeting Veronica.

"There was nothing wrong with your decision, you know that," Thomas said. "We're always here if you ever need anything. Plus, you got Veronica here to help." She leaned in and took Ben's arm, smiling.

"Well, actually, Thomas and I have got to get back to our places," Lincoln said, shoving his hands in his pockets. "It's getting kind of late. We've been up since six."

"All right, well, you guys get going then," Ben said. "Don't be a stranger."

Thomas and Lincoln walked out the door as Ben and Veronica waved. They hopped back into the Rover and took off. The sun was low on the horizon with crickets chirping. Thomas reclined his seat and looked out the window, watching the streetlights zip by.

"Sometimes I worry about Ben," he said. "It seems like his wife and kids are the only thing he has keeping him together."

"Well, I mean, they're his family," Lincoln said.

"Yeah, I get that. Plenty of times when he was slinging guns with us, he always had that vibe that he was extremely lonely. Just happy for him that those days are done."

"Yeah, with the amount of missions that we flew and led, he deserved his big break for sure."

"That is true. Gotta hand it to him, Thaw, I envy him from time to time. I wish I had a wife to call my own. But that's why I have hobbies to keep me company," Thomas said, kicking his feet on the dashboard.

"What do you think is gonna happen to that sword we recovered for Roland Industries?" Lincoln asked.

"What do you think?" Thomas asked. "The same thing Clinton has always done. He'll dissect the shit out of it and see if it's worthy of weaponizing it. But something was off about the blade: it felt as if there was a prime reason Gorroff went through all that trouble to get it." Thomas turned to look at the road ahead.

"We just gotta take our time with this one," Lincoln said. "Roland Industries has treated us very well over the past few years. It's only fair we let them handle this one. The question is what the hell would they do with a sword? It's the twenty-first century, not the Middle Ages."

"I can't wait till I hear what's gonna happen with the Souls of Death. With their leader gone, it's only a matter of time until they disperse and we never hear from them again."

"I wouldn't say that. Something tells me we're going to see them again, really soon," Lincoln said.

"Way to foreshadow something awful, Thaw." Thomas laughed. He slapped Lincoln's shoulder.

They rolled up to Thomas's very large house with columns in the front reaching high to the two-story roof. The windows were black, and there were no lights on. Roland Industries paid their soldiers well. They would pay them more if they found something that would benefit the company. The duo found everything from little scraps of plans and blueprints from the Souls of Death to new cars that Arabians built to win the war effort. Roland employees were living large and loving every second of it.

A lone streetlamp glowed brightly in the night over the Rover. Thomas leaned over and hugged Lincoln. They bid each other goodbye as Thomas got out of the car and shut the door behind him. Once Thomas was safely inside, Lincoln drove off, enjoying a moment of peace on his way home.

He gazed upon the oncoming streetlights above him, passing by like indistinct memories. He felt the gravel below the vehicle moving like the current of the sea. He thought about all the events leading up to this moment and how grateful he was to serve his country by fighting alongside his friends. People had always come and gone so quickly in his life. He always tried to cherish moments with them because he sensed that they wouldn't last forever.

Sometimes he would think, *Is this all I am?* or *Can I not be better?* He had served his country well, but he always wanted to push himself in ways most people never dreamed possible. On the outside, he was always a strong man, but on the inside, he was often unsure.

His eyes stayed glued on the road as he lingered on one thought in particular: *Why was that sword so important?* He thought about

Gorroff's family. He tried to remember the feeling of families receiving the news that their loved one had passed away. He hated that part of his job.

But the sword was even stranger. The markings on the blade looked ancient, as if it was crafted by wise men of the distant past. "What year was it from? How did it get there?" Maybe Clinton knew these answers. He didn't know if it was right to hand over care of an antique that people had died over.

As Lincoln approached his house, he realized he was exhausted. His house was in a much more rural area than Thomas's. He lived by a peaceful farm surrounded by cornfields. His house was a nice little home he built himself, two stories with red shutters and a detached garage. He loved the peace and quiet of living far away from everyone else. The garage was abnormally large. He had bright neon signs from all over the world when he traveled displayed for anyone to see if they came inside.

He loved his man-cave and thought about it as he drove his SUV down the long gravel trail that led to his house. He parked the Rover and stepped out, closing the door behind him. He looked up to the sky and admired the simple beauty of the colorful clouds. The sun had nearly set, so the sky was filled with swaths of red and orange. He walked into his house and locked the door behind him. He had only one thought on his mind: sleep.

★ ★ ★

Meanwhile back in Iraq, scientists were working around the clock, scanning the mysterious sword in the stone with a number of machines. Machines that were from the top minds of the world. They found absolutely nothing. They were starting to think maybe it was best if they gave up. But they were scared to give up because they would have to answer to Clinton. Reporting that they couldn't find anything would be career homicide.

Clinton could be very temperamental. He was an intellectual who made clinical decisions based on available research, but he could become unhinged when he was told no. The scientists stood assembled in a large hangar—called BULL for Base for Ultrastructural Logistics Liberation—with equipment that reached the ceiling. That was where the world's top minds went to calculate data and converse amongst themselves. Their sole purpose was to find ancient artifacts and prisoners of war and bring them home by any means necessary. The scientists crowded around the sword, taking notes on their clipboards while computers calculated its energy. Their concentration was broken when Clinton barged through the door and approached them angrily.

"It's been almost twenty-seven hours and still nothing yet? I knew I should've hired better people," Clinton said, rubbing his temples.

"Actually, sir, we've found something," one of the men said. He spoke softly and hugged his clipboard in fear.

"Don't talk," Clinton said, holding his palm toward the man. "Soldiers have almost died getting this little hunk of junk and the best you give me is just one goddamn thing? You mean to tell me I wasted my time getting this just for one little blip to pop up on your radar?"

"The power in the building seems to decrease and the lights flicker every time we try to drill into the rock shielding us from freeing it," the man said. "There's a 57 percent decrease in power, to be exact."

"I don't give a . . . wait, it's taking away our power?" Clinton asked. His jaw grew slack.

"That's our guess, but this thing has a certain way of reacting to blades that touch it. Every time we try to get close to it or touch it, it sends out an energy pulse," the man said. The other scientists' eyes drifted toward Clinton for a response. They were pleased to see he was intrigued.

"Show me."

CHAPTER 3

THE MEN WORKED DILIGENTLY TO remove the wreckage from the explosion. The Souls of Death were looking for their leader, Hakim Gorroff, in the debris. They held out hope that he could still lead the group to victory against the Americans that had taken the sword. The clouds above were black and darkened the scene. The men carried an array of tools such as shovels, blades, and crowbars to get through the rubble.

One soldier was sifting through the metal shrapnel of their shredded base. While shoveling a piece of a gun turret, he discovered a hand poking through the pile of twisted metal. The soldier screamed for help, and the rest of the team turned and ran to him. They tripped and struggled to make their way up the pile without falling back down. When they finally reached the very top, they stopped and stared at the hand in horror. Several men grabbed hold of it and pulled it from the wreckage. Finally, with one last pull, the rest of the body emerged. They heaved harder and froze when they saw the body of their leader, battered and bloodied, his face burned almost beyond recognition.

Blood trickled down from his hairline, and his eyes were black; blue bruises covered his mouth and ears. His clothes were shredded. The men called out for his son, Raheem Gorroff, who sprinted from the other side of the wreckage to investigate what had happened. He ran up the mound of metal and looked at his father, his mouth gaping as he leaned down and touched his father's cheek. Rage flowed through his veins like venom. He slowly stood up and looked at the men.

He reached into his pocket and pulled a revolver out of his side holster. "Who was in charge of this operation?"

"I was," one of the soldiers said. The man's hands trembled with fear. "We were taken by storm. It was an assault on our territory. They will pay, I promise you that."

"You see, I just don't understand how hard it is for you people to do one damn job around here without the Americans stalking you," Raheem said, smiling. "Have you at least investigated where the explosion originated?"

"Our forensics team determined that the SUV gas tank was the source of the initial explosion, and they found the remains of an extremely long-range bullet lodged in the wreckage of the SUV."

Raheem was overcome with rage: there was only a handful of men that could have pulled off a shot like this. "Lincoln Thaw. It's been a long time indeed."

BANG! The door crashed off its hinges as the American squadron stormed into the consulate building. Raheem felt a sudden rush of panic overtake him.

"The Americans found us! They're here!" Javid screamed.

"Take whatever you can! Wipe the hard drives!" Raheem yelled. "We need backup in here!" he shouted into the radio.

The consulate building erupted with screams and gunfire downstairs.

Javid grabbed the pistol from the wooden desk and loaded it in anticipation. Just as he cocked it, the door busted open, as numerous lasers fell onto his chest.

The American leader kept his rifle trained on Javid.

"Put down the weapon! Face to the ground. Hands behind your head! Now!" the American soldier commanded.

Javid's hand shook with overwhelming fear. He raised the pistol slowly.

The American soldier shot Javid in the chest.

"You son of a bitch!" Raheem screamed. He ran to the pistol on the ground.

One of the other soldiers tackled Raheem to the ground.

"Lock this place down and radio for assistance. Tell headquarters we found Raheem Gorroff. We've neutralized the threat here."

The American leader flipped the night-vision goggles upward to look Raheem in the eyes. The patch on his suit identified him as L. Thaw.

"You're coming with us, Gorroff."

Raheem snapped his mind back to the present and, in one swift motion, whipped his pistol in front of the soldier's face and pulled the trigger. The soldier's body fell, lifeless, into the pile of wreckage. Raheem holstered his revolver and clipped the holster shut.

"Take my father and do what you can to stitch him back up." He turned around and walked down the wreckage, stepping over his father's body. If they didn't get this man to a hospital bed soon, they knew they would experience Raheem's rage firsthand; two men picked him up and carried him to the nearest sick bay.

Raheem had always been temperamental. He was raised in a hostile family. His father shot and killed Raheem's mother right in front of him just to prove a point: no one could talk down to him. However, Raheem always wanted to impress his father, and he always managed to do so. He had killed an immeasurable number of people, including so many American soldiers that the US specifically targeted him. He made sure that he left a wake of death everywhere he traveled. No matter what or who he encountered, he was as ruthless as his father.

★ ★ ★

Raheem awoke with a start the next morning. Gunfire filled the air and the glass window in his quarters shattered. He immediately jumped out of bed and grabbed his pistol. He readied his weapon and stealthily looked out the window.

Outside, he saw people in shredded combat gear with semi-destroyed gas masks, eyeholes cracked from the inside. They were all firing at his cot, which was pelted with a storm of bullets. He panicked and fled out of his tent, firing back at some of the men. He ran up a large sand dune and turned around to see that more of them were running from the horizon, firing and sprinting toward him. Suddenly, he felt hands on his shoulders, and before he knew it, he was thrown down into the sand.

When he was finally able to look up, he saw that more of the mysterious gas-masked men had reached the top of the hill. He rose and fired at the oncoming men, killing several in a hailstorm of bullets. But as more fell to the ground, a new wave of soldiers took their places. Eventually, his gun jammed, and he tossed it to the ground. He decided to use hand-to-hand combat, running up to one of the men and punching him in the face. To his bewilderment, he felt a searing pain in his right leg.

He was being swarmed from different directions now. It grew hard for him to breathe, and his ribs were crushed under the weight.

A moment later, he jolted out of his bed and coughed violently. Moonlight shined on his sweat-stained sheets. Raheem scanned the room to ensure he was actually safe. He sighed in relief.

It was just another nightmare, he thought as the adrenaline rush subsided.

Psychiatrists had given him medication since he was a child. Physical wounds were easy to heal, but psychological wounds were never truly resolved. When he was a child, a clan of mysterious gas-masked men raided his village and attacked his dad. They beat him brutally and then did the same to his son. They threw Raheem into a fire, burning his back. They were going to end the child's life had it not been for the Souls of Death raining fire down upon the masked men.

"My name is Raheem Gorroff. I'm the leader of the Souls of Death. It is three in the morning. I am in control," he repeated to himself.

The moonlight loomed above him, as if salvation was creeping into his room, offering him freedom from panic. He stood in the center of his room in silence, listening to the creatures that lurked in the darkness nearby. He closed his eyes and thought of his dad. His father loved him, yes, but he was always very stern. He tried his best to raise his son to make him tough enough to face the world without fear.

Hakim always had a cold soul but an even colder heart to test his son.

Raheem ran out of his tent to the medical bay to check on his father. The sand seemed to pull him under as he ran. The night was strangely calm. The Souls of Death were almost always attacked, but tonight was different. It was as if fate had given them a break from the mayhem to let them breathe.

The medical bay was nothing more than a four-poled tent covered in a tarpaulin, with five sick beds and limited medical supplies. He looked down at his unconscious father on his bed with a blanket over him. Raheem bent down next to him.

Suddenly, Hakim's eyes shot open. He grabbed his son's collar and screamed.

"What happened? Where am I?" He thrashed around the bed as if he was having a seizure.

Raheem quickly shook his father's shoulder to wake him from his trance. Hakim calmed down as his heart rate normalized. Hakim slowly turned his head and looked into his son's eyes.

"They took . . . the sword—" He struggled to speak but coughed violently.

"I know, Father. They will pay for this, I promise. I will scour the earth to find it and bring it back to the motherland. We will be victorious."

"Bring it back and . . . unlock its—" He coughed again. He turned to his son once more. "Bring the sword back to me, son. It's imperative."

"I will kill the man who did this to you. No one comes to our territory, destroys our land, and burns my father. I shall kill the American who almost killed you."

Hakim looked at him and closed his eyes. He shifted his head over back to the center of the pillow and spoke. "Do what you must, Raheem. But remember, if something happens to you, you're on your own."

Raheem nodded.

"I understand." He raised his body and was about to walk away from the medical bay when his father spoke again.

"His name was Lincoln. Lincoln Thaw. If you can find him, he's probably back in America by now," Hakim said with his eyes still closed. He coughed again and began to wheeze.

Raheem stared into the night sky, filling with rage. He turned to his father. "Where in America?"

Hakim winced and reached into his pocket. He pulled out a piece of paper. Raheem snatched the paper out of his hand.

"What's this?" Raheem asked.

Hakim opened his eyes. "After we took the sword, we were going to bomb the Americans at these coordinates. But if you can infiltrate their base and steal their aircraft, you can not only get the sword, but kill Lincoln Thaw as well."

Raheem looked at him and smiled.

"Consider him dead, then," he said.

He turned and sprinted back to his tent to grab his supplies. If he was going to steal a mighty aircraft, then he had to be prepared. He grabbed his black leather jacket and goggles to protect him from sandstorms, and his combat knife and pistol. He was determined to be ready for anything or anyone that came his way. He grabbed his bag of explosives and weapons specially used for being on the actual battlefield. He threw on his hood so no one could recognize him and took off to his battered Jeep at the edge of their makeshift camp. He turned the key and slammed on the gas, disappearing into the night.

★ ★ ★

The stars seemed to guide him to the right place as he saw a field of lights in the distance. Raheem floored it as the motor roared. He gradually saw the base clearer. He lightly tapped on the brake to avoid detection. This was the danger zone for him now. If they heard him, he might as well be dead.

He was only a mile away from the gargantuan reinforced metal wall separating the outside world from BULL. He grabbed his knapsack, one of his few possessions from childhood. He ran and saw a guard standing by the entrance. Hiding behind a column connected to the wall, Raheem closed his eyes to concentrate.

He removed his combat knife from his belt and peered from behind the column. Raheem raised his knife slowly and cocked his arm then quickly threw it with precision at the guard standing forty feet away. The knife plunged into the soldier's neck, and he fell wordlessly. Raheem retreated and held his hand out, activating his blade retraction gauntlet. The knife flew out of the deceased guard's neck and landed in Raheem's hand.

Raheem leaped silently into the air. He landed on the second guard's back and wrapped his legs around his arms. He applied pressure, covered the man's mouth, and plunged the knife into his neck, twisting it until he was dead. He fell to the ground, and Raheem jumped off. He put the knife back in his belt and picked up one of the guards. He pulled him over to the hand scanner and waited patiently for the scanner to authenticate him. A computerized voice authorized his clearance.

"*Handprint Identification Approved.*"

The twin doors slowly opened. He smiled under the hood and ran into the doors with growing confidence. He knew there was no going back. He passed through the door of no return. He raced forward as the search lights from the security towers above scanned for allied jets. He ran until he felt his lungs give out. His target: the runway where jets took off for destinations around the world. He reached into his belt and pulled out a grenade, holding it close to his head.

"I will avenge my father. I will avenge my homeland. The ones who do me injustice will pay for their sins."

Several flagmen stood on the runway in the distance. He took one last deep breath and sprinted toward them. Under the cover of darkness, he completely surprised them, grabbing one by the neck and snapping it in one motion. He lunged at the other flagman, knocking him to the ground. Raheem took out his knife and thrust it into the man's chest then eyed him with a crazed look.

He turned and sprinted toward an oncoming jet in the middle of the runway. The jet was a quarter mile down the runway and nearing lift-off speed. The pilot panicked and immediately pulled the lever to lift off. The pilot succeeded, but Raheem tossed a grenade just before the jet escaped.

"J-17 to Houston, we have a—" Suddenly, the grenade detonated, and the jet exploded in a massive fireball. Roland Air Traffic Control watched in horror. The team of air traffic control sat in silence, wondering what had just happened.

"Francis, what are you waiting for?" one of the controllers screamed. "Sound the alarm. Do it, goddamn it!"

He ran over and slammed the alarm button. The siren screeched through the tower and across the airfield, reverberating through the floor. The director of the team took the intercom.

"Code red. I repeat, code red. This is not a drill. We have an intruder. Find him and arm yourselves!"

Raheem heard the alarm and knew he had to find a jet and take off as soon as possible. He ran into three guards that came from behind one of the buildings and brought out their guns. They fired everything they had and actually managed to shoot Raheem in the shoulder. He winced in pain and kept running.

★ ★ ★

Clinton was in BULL signing a few papers regarding the sword in the stone being moved to a classified, secure location. He stopped writing and listened to the faraway clamor. He heard muffled gunshots and screaming. He was about to look out the window when it shattered. Raheem burst through it like a bullet.

Raheem landed on his feet and stared at Clinton. He was bloodied and limping. He wore his goggles, but they had blood smeared over the lenses. His hair was now a jumbled mess. He instantly shot his arm up and held a pistol he stole from the guards in Clinton's face. Clinton froze with fear.

"Give me the sword, or so help me, I will pull the trigger and find someone else to give it to me," Raheem said.

Clinton's heart raced. He began to hyperventilate.

"I'll show you the sword. If you kill me, you're saying goodbye to a lot more information you may need," Clinton said, trying to control his breathing. "What's your name?"

"Raheem Gorroff, and I'm here to bring justice for my father. That sword rightfully belongs to my people. Lead me to it." Raheem gripped the trigger with his finger.

"All right, just follow me. No need to get hasty here. We want the same thing."

"Move!" Raheem screamed.

Clinton walked to the door and opened it. The sword was connected to countless machines in the hangar. They measured a variety of telemetric readings such as radiation leaks, electrical currents, and even particle acceleration anomalies. He felt the pistol pressed against his back and knew he had to come up with something fast or this might be it. If he overloaded the machines, they would combust, giving him the chance to run away and survive.

They walked down the flashing hallway. Power in the base had been compromised by the blast, leaving parts of the base dark. They walked further down the dim hallway until they reached one lonely yellow door at the end. Raheem picked up his pace, forcing Clinton to walk faster as well. Clinton opened the door, revealing the hangar to Raheem, who gasped with amazement.

"Now guide me to where my weapon is," Raheem demanded.

In anger, he shoved Clinton to the floor. Clinton got up slowly and straightened his brown suit and red tie. He glared at the intruder before turning and walking to the sword. He heard Raheem close behind him. The hangar was losing power fast. The antimatter lights from the ceiling were flickering as they walked through a maze of machinery and hardware until he stopped and stood in front of the platform that held the sword in the stone.

Raheem admired the beauty of the sword. He walked closer to it and dropped his gun to his side. Clinton took a step back in retreat, but Raheem heard him and quickly pointed the gun at him. Impulsively, he pulled the trigger once and sent a blast into his arm. Clinton screamed in pain and bent down, gritting his teeth.

"The next bullet is going through your head, you American swine," Raheem said, his finger twitching on the trigger.

As Clinton gasped for air, he noticed the sword starting to glow, slowly growing brighter and more radiant. Raheem, startled, pulled the trigger for the second and final time. The bullet grazed Clinton and ricocheted off the sword's hilt. The whole hangar suddenly turned into a white blur. Raheem dropped his gun and shielded his eyes from the blinding light. The two screamed in agony as Clinton's wounds were suddenly healed. His eyes glowed gold like the sword itself.

Clinton's head filled with visions. A man stood in golden armor swinging the same blade that was stuck in the stone. Next he saw the sword being dropped into lava, but it didn't melt. The blade impaled itself into the ground as it succumbed to the lava. Now Clinton knew how the sword fused with the stone. A third vision was of an unknown man dressed in all black holding the sword.

Raheem did not receive any visions. Rather, his body was overtaken by an unbearable pain. He felt the bones in his legs shift and move. His arms tingled in excruciating pain. His nerves felt as if they were on fire. He tried to look at his limbs, but he could only see a bright white light. His screaming stopped when his throat started to burn. It felt as if something was under his flesh. He flung his arms to his side and screamed once more into the air, only to be blown away while the base was consumed with hellfire.

The hangar formerly known as BULL was leveled to the ground in an instant, with ash everywhere. All machines, equipment, and belongings were vaporized. Clinton slowly regained consciousness and opened his eyes. He stood in horror as he realized the base was completely gone. His wounds were gone now, too, and he stood in a clean suit. It was as if the bullet never hit him. He was standing in the middle of the rubble. He turned to his right and found the stranger standing up as well with no wounds and his clothing restored to its former state. They stared at each other, completely dumbfounded.

"What the hell?" Clinton muttered. His hands shook from both fear and trauma. He noticed something shiny peeking out of the rubble.

The golden sword was out of its rocky confines. The entire sword pulsed with light, as if it were trying to get his attention. Clinton's gaze was distracted when Raheem ran up to him and punched him, knocking him to the ground. He winced in pain as he hit the ground and didn't even bother to get up.

Clinton looked up and noticed Raheem standing by the sword with a twisted smile on his face. Raheem bent down slowly and grabbed the handle. He stood up and admired the beauty of the blade. He saw his own reflection and noticed Clinton on the ground, turning to face him.

He walked over to Clinton and raised the sword; Clinton closed his eyes and raised a hand to protect himself.

As soon as Raheem brought the blade upon him, Clinton felt a puff of air and a loud, warping sound. He then heard the sword dropping to the ground. He slowly opened his eyes to see that Raheem had disappeared, gone without a trace.

Clinton shot up from the rubble and frantically looked around the open space. All he could see was the blackness of night and the golden sword lying on the ground. He bent down and picked it up. This time, when he looked at the blade, he noticed something different: a reflection that wasn't his own. He saw a vision of the future.

It was Lincoln Thaw holding the sword and appearing triumphant from battle.

An angelic, feminine voice spoke in his head: *"You are the Guardian of Excalibur. Should evil arise and take control, look for the place which holds the scroll."*

The reflection in the sword returned to that of his own. He instantly looked away and dropped the sword by his waist. He looked around, still wondering where Raheem had gone. Now he had a mission with a paranormal and astounding past. Clinton felt as if a section of his brain had been unlocked. He knew everything about the sword, where it came from, why it was made, even its purpose. Clinton knew that, with this sword—Excalibur—he could advance any and all weapons for the betterment of mankind. He felt lightheaded as he lost consciousness.

CHAPTER 4

A LOUD RINGING FILLED THE night air as Lincoln jolted awake from a deep sleep. He always hated to answer a call while he was half-awake. His eyes were glued shut, and he fumbled for the phone. His vision was blurry until he focused on the moonlight piercing his window. He turned his head toward the direction of the noise. He finally spotted his old-fashioned landline phone ringing. He moaned angrily and reached for it.

"Thaw residence," he mumbled.

"It's Thomas."

"Thomas, its four in the morning—" Thaw started.

"Lincoln, this is serious. BULL was just demolished. There's nothing left, and the sword is out of the stone. Clinton's the only survivor."

Lincoln shot up out of bed. "What the hell do you mean? What happened?"

"Clinton says a guy destroyed a jet and infiltrated the base, killing a few soldiers. Their families are mourning. A clean-up crew is on the way to retrieve the remains. But the sword . . . Clinton is sure acting weird about it."

"Who was responsible? You didn't answer my question."

"Clinton says it was one guy. That had to have been one pissed-off dude," Thomas said.

"How the hell did just one guy get through professionally trained guards and the world's top technology?"

"That's what we're trying to find out. I was just notified, so I'm just as confused as you right now."

"He was probably a hacker for the Souls of Death trying to get back at us. Where is he?"

"He's apparently gone missing, according to Clinton. He says that apparently he 'vanished' into thin air."

"Vanished into thin air?" Lincoln repeated. He was starting to think maybe Clinton had finally let his imagination get the better of him. "Keep me informed, Thomas. We have no idea what's gonna happen next."

"Will do. You do the same." Thomas hung up.

Lincoln knew Clinton wasn't all that crazy, and he was generally too rational to act weird. If anything, he was fascinated by it and wanted to know more. But none of this made sense. It wasn't possible for one man to penetrate their base, much less totally obliterate it.

He couldn't sleep for the rest of the night. At six a.m., he got into his car and drove out of his farm, clutching the wheel and feeling the gravel churn beneath him. He drove onto the main road for miles before he finally reached Ben's house. His ears perked up when he heard the words "explosions" and "one man" on the car radio. He increased the volume and listened closely.

"Now here's an exclusive. Late last night in Iraq, the base formerly known as BULL, built by Roland Industries, was obliterated in a terrorist attack. A total of six hundred people were killed due to this horrendous act of violence. The only survivor is Vice President of Roland Industries, James Clinton. There is speculation that another survivor was with Clinton but fled the scene. Numerous observers are saying he ran away to avoid getting caught by the military."

He turned down the radio and muttered to himself, "They didn't say anything about the sword." He finally reached Ben's house and parked. He walked up to the house and noticed that Ben was at the front door.

"Hey, Lincoln, what brings you here?" Ben asked after opening the door.

"It's BULL. It's gone, Ben. Everything except for Clinton and the sword."

Ben stopped dead in his tracks.

"What do you mean, gone? That's impossible."

"Do you mind if we talk inside?" Lincoln asked. They walked inside and sat down at the dinner table. The kids were at school, and Veronica was grocery shopping. Lincoln explained everything he knew, from the base exploding to the sword out of the stone. He even told him what Thomas said about the man disappearing into thin air. Ben was at a loss for words.

"I don't even know what to say. He just disappeared? How's that even possible? He couldn't have gotten very far if they were surrounded by rubble."

"That's what I'm thinking," Lincoln responded.

"So the sword just . . . broke out of the stone? Honestly sounds like Excalibur to me."

"At this point, I'd believe that. Everything about the sword adds up."

"What do you mean? It's actually Excalibur?"

"Think about it. Why would the Souls of Death try to hide it? Their leader was told that it was smuggled away during World War II and again during the Cold War. Who knows how many other ones as well?"

"Then why would it be in Iraq? Shouldn't it be in England where the myths originated?"

"Your guess is as good as mine. That sword's been raising issues ever since we found the damn thing in the desert," Lincoln said. He got up to get a glass of water.

"But it's just a myth, right? It'd be ludicrous to think that it's actually real. Just a bunch of hocus pocus bullshit, right?" Ben asked.

Lincoln fiddled around with his glass. He finally turned to face Ben.

"We need to rule out the impossible. I have to investigate and see what the hell is going on with this sword." Lincoln pressed the refrigerator button to dispense water. "I have to know for sure now."

"If you're doing this, I'm going with you," Ben said. "I know I've been out of the loop for some time now, but I have to protect my country."

Lincoln almost spat out the water and put down the glass.

"There's no way you're throwing yourself in the middle of this. Don't you remember what happened the last time you showed yourself in front of Roland Industries? In front of Clinton?"

Ben was always a go-getter to help his friends, but it almost led to him getting hurt multiple times. The last time he did that, he was lucky to get away with his leg reattached to his hip. The wounds healed within a week thanks to Roland Industries. They rushed him to the nearest hospital after getting him back from the desert. Shortly afterward, Clinton scolded him for being unreliable and practically acted like he was dead to him.

"I get that. I know, but you need to find the man who destroyed the base and figure out where the sword came from. Face it, you need me." Ben stood and faced Lincoln squarely in the eye. Lincoln sighed and closed his eyes to think about the poor decision he was about to make. He knew that if he said yes, Ben would be put in harm's way, but if he said no, he'd just come anyway. He opened his eyes.

"You wanna come? Fine. Only if you stick to me like flies on shit. You understand?"

"Yes, I understand. Can we get Thomas along for this as well?" Ben asked.

"That was the plan. Let's get him and head out. I can only imagine what Roland Industries is doing with it right now."

★ ★ ★

Raheem's vision was blurry. He saw only stars and blackness. His vision cleared up after a minute, and he felt nothing but sheer terror.

He was in space. He saw nothing but a vast, endless array of stars. The blackness only added to the fear of something coming from the darkness to approach him. He whipped his head in every direction. This made no logical sense. How did he end up there? Was someone or something watching him? Was there a reason he was there? He noticed he was floating in space. How was he even breathing? He started to panic.

Until he was pulled into a wormhole that disfigured his body.

His screaming grew irrelevant. He closed his eyes and waited for his doom. When he emerged from the hostile wormhole, he found himself amongst company: the company of worlds. Raheem drifted along a current that was moving very slowly. He saw an endless array of globes within other globes. Stars were glowing in every single one. Every world was trapped by another circle, which had another orb containing it. In the middle of it all was nothing but an endless black tunnel. It appeared that the harder he looked, the more orbs he saw.

"Am I dead?" he asked himself. Raheem's voice echoed through the endless nothingness. He looked at an approaching star and held up his hand to catch it. It slowly floated to him, and he somehow found peace within this light. It was the embodiment of comfort. He sensed that it would be okay if he touched it. The light finally reached his hand, and he grabbed hold of it. He could not feel it, but he could feel the aura surrounding it. He could feel warmth and the strange feeling of hope. It was as if fear and all negative emotions were fading away. A smile appeared on his face, and he felt nothing could ever take that feeling away.

Another star drifted toward him, and he let go of the one he held, which drifted away. He reached out and grabbed the new star and felt the opposite of what he was feeling before. Suddenly, he felt immense anger, sadness, fear, and hatred. He let go because the star's aura was too strong for him. A tear streamed down his face. He was about to cry out for help, but a voice interrupted his thoughts.

"Do you understand now?" a beautiful, female voice asked throughout the vast blackness. The voice seemed to echo throughout eternity. Raheem's heart raced.

"Who's there?" he asked, whipping his head in every direction.

"I'm everywhere, everything, and all there will ever be. I am Aura, watcher of the Multi-Precinct."

The voice spoke with a bright flashing light overtaking his vision. Raheem shielded his eyes from the blinding light. There appeared to be the faint silhouette of a humanoid figure taking shape. He saw limbs growing from the side and legs concurrently forming. The figure seemed female and glorious.

Her eyes glowed gold, and she flashed a calming smile. Her long blue and gold hair drifted in the antigravity cosmos of space-time. Her body was pitch black and embodied stars from every corner of the galaxy. She was vibrant with natural starlight as she floated over to him. A golden square pulsated on her neck every time she spoke. It seemed to hypnotize Raheem as she approached him. He knew that he could do nothing to this thing from the vastness of space. The closer she got, the more he could visibly make out the features of her eyes. They were the equivalent of million-dollar jewels. It seemed as though every shade of gold rested within her pupils.

"Do not be afraid of me, Raheem," she said. "I know that you mean to take back what was taken from you."

Raheem instantly lowered his arms as his eyes grew in shock.

"What is this place? Please tell me how I got here," he asked in desperation.

The mystical being put a hand on his shoulder. "As I have stated before, Raheem, my name is Aura. I am one of the last of my species that has guarded the Multiverse for quintillions of years. Since long before humanity was manifested. You and I are in what is known as the Multi-Precinct. For every action has an opposite reaction, which creates another Earth where you made the opposite decision. You humans refer to this as science fiction, am I correct?"

"Yes," he muttered. "What exactly are you?"

"I come from a planet birthed into existence trillions of years before the first human created fire. My home planet had always been present and remained nameless for millions of generations due to our ceaseless advancements in our psychological and physiological states. We were a gentle race that welcomed new beings into the universe we shared. Our kind was boundless in knowledge and all powerful in the reaction of new life forms.

"As time progressed," she continued, "we were able to unlock the universe's most gargantuan obstacle: the ability to achieve unlimited potential cosmic omniscience, a task that millions of our past generations attempted to achieve but simply could not. Eventually, as our species grew older, we discovered quantum manipulation, interdimensional foresight, instant teleportation, and omnipotence. Inevitably, the ability to foresee millions of outcomes showed us the dark path toward our planet's end. We embraced it and accepted that as our fate. The planet slowly became a lifeless wasteland of despair that forced us to individually leave the atmosphere of our home planet."

Raheem focused on one star far in the distance in between two other Earths. Aura raised her arm, and the golden square on her neck glowed brightly. Space around them seemed to move at the speed of light as they rushed to the star in a matter of seconds. Before Raheem could blink, they were standing in a field of rich green grass spread out as far as he could see. The sun shone bright and high above them, and the Milky Way stretched out across the sky. Outer space was visible, so he could see a distant world that looked like another Earth, sitting in the sky like a titan. The sun quickly fell behind the horizon as darkness overtook them. He turned to Aura, who now hovered over the grass with closed eyes.

"You are standing on an alternate Earth, in which living creatures never came to be, and the Earth remained untouched for billions of years. No humans to claim the land and no wars to demolish nature's beauty."

"I could stay here forever," Raheem said.

Aura's square on her neck grew bright once more, and she raised a hand. A moment later, they teleported to another place. The space around them seemed to flash by at the speed of light. Raheem was suddenly standing in the middle of a crowd of people in Times Square. He was confused. "How is this any different from the world I reside in?"

"Observe the television screen, Raheem," Aura said.

Raheem watched the closest monitor through a window in an electronics store. It showed a female news anchor with the headline below her reading "25th Anniversary of Failed Terror Attacks on World Trade Center." Raheem stepped back and fell to his knees in shock. He couldn't believe what he was hearing.

"Don't you see?" Aura asked. "Your father was never born to assist Osama Bin Laden in the 9/11 attacks. Thousands of lives were saved as a result."

"Show me just one more example," Raheem said. "I understand now what kind of place you safeguard. But I need one more alternate Earth. An Earth where I successfully killed that man."

"As you wish," Aura said. She raised a hand so that they suddenly warped across space before stopping abruptly in the same spot of Raheem's last memory. He saw Clinton lying on the ground, struggling to get up. He looked over and watched another version of himself bending down and picking up the sword. It was strange seeing another version of himself, almost like watching a home video from an alternate reality. He stopped walking and stood right in front of Clinton. He wore a horrified expression as the blade rose higher. Raheem watched in anticipation.

"This is where you die," the parallel Raheem said as he slashed the sword to the ground, killing Clinton at once. Blood streamed down his face. His lifeless eyes stared at the sky above. Raheem's face was covered in his blood, as was the sword. Raheem couldn't stop watching the malicious event unfolding before him. Suddenly, everything around him changed, and they warped back in between the infinite Earths. Raheem seemed irate to have been pulled from this moment.

"You see that? That's all I planned on doing to the guy," he said to Aura.

"Why do you seek the elimination of your fellow man? You should be helping each other instead of killing each other. My analysis of the matter is that as humans, you have the basic nature to do that. It's truly despairing."

"You don't understand where I've come from. The places I've been, the people I've seen, and most importantly, how I was raised. My earth is a nasty place full of parasites that must be put in their place before they grow into an infestation. Humans have a long track record of causing world wars and mass panic. The gas chambers of the Holocaust, Pearl harbor, Operation Desert Storm, and 9/11 are all products of war. I was raised to take vengeance upon the people that took from me, and Allah help me, I will return the sword to my father. Even if I have to go through you."

"Your hostility proves that you do not yet have wisdom enough to fully grasp the power of the Multi-Precinct. That said, I abide by the requirements of Excalibur and its demands. If this law wasn't in effect, I would've cast you out."

"What do you mean?" Raheem asked.

"You are the first human in seven hundred years that has been able to cross between worlds with me. You have the capability of interdimensional transport and the strength of titans. This gift is completely up to you to use. Reluctantly, I must let you have these powers because it wasn't me who granted you this gift. It was Excalibur."

"With this, I can get the sword and kill whoever gets in my way," Raheem said, a smile creeping over his face. "The one named Thaw is first on my list. The only thing I wanted to do in my life was to strike fear in my enemies and punish those who oppose me. This is my chance to finally prove myself worthy and show my father that

I am capable of great things." Raheem looked down at his arm as it started to glow a bright, almost gold, light that seemed to make his arm fade from existence. His other arm was fading away, too, and his legs were growing translucent.

"What's happening to me?" he asked. "What is this?"

"No human can stay in the Multi-Precinct for long. I bid you farewell, Mr. Gorroff. I'll be watching." In that moment, Raheem faded to nothing. Aura stared at the spot Raheem had occupied, staring into the foreboding, infinite Earths.

CHAPTER 5

LINCOLN, THOMAS, AND BEN WERE in downtown Norfolk, the heart of Roland Industries. Back in 2009, the company bought half the city as it was about to be renovated. They promised they would not only help with remaking Norfolk, but they would also make it the company's main headquarters.

It worked, and the great skyscraper now stood tall above the rest of the city. *The Virginia Pilot*'s earnings and readership went up 8.9 percent. Roland Industries had become larger than Google, which it purchased in 2010. They held every piece of equipment or technology that might be available in the future or might be pushed aside for further testing or prototype advancement.

Lincoln, Thomas, and Ben stood in the basement level, which held the sword behind a glass dome. Scientists in white lab coats surrounded the dome, taking all sorts of notes and studies. It was recovered with Clinton's unconscious body. The trio stood right in front of the dome, thanks to their military clearance. A scientist named Leonard Pascale spoke with them about the incident.

"What I'm saying is that I don't know if we can actually touch this. It may be a bomb activated by thermal touch."

"What about Clinton?" Thomas asked. "I heard he was in here. Could we see him?"

"No visitors are allowed right now. He's in critical condition. He's been coming in and out of consciousness."

"Did someone hit him? Was he shot or something?" Ben asked.

"That's what we're trying to figure out. He's shaking too violently for us to do anything."

"Have you tried tranquilizing him? Normally, that puts them right to sleep."

"We have, but it doesn't tire him out. The most it does is slow his heart rate, but he burns right through the damn fluid and his heart rate climbs until he flat lines. Strange thing is he hasn't died of hyperventilation yet." Lenny held his clipboard and looked over his notes.

"But what has the sword been doing, huh?"

"The sword gives off this energy that spikes every ten minutes," Lenny said. "It increases 10 percent and fluctuates before decreasing back to zero. The paranormal thing about it is every time the energy spikes, Clinton has a massive seizure."

"Do you think . . . ?" Ben started to ask.

"I guess some myths have a way of catching up with present day," Lincoln said. Suddenly, a voice from down the hallway made nearly everyone jump out of their skin.

"I need assistance with Clinton, now!" a doctor cried. Several scientists on the floor ran down the hallway to help. Each immediately drew the same conclusion. The sword's energy fluctuation patterns matched those of Clinton's seizures. They were somehow connected.

The trio ran with the scientists, hoping to blend with the crowd in order to get into Clinton's room. But they were quickly pushed out of the way. The door was closed and latched shut to prevent them from entering. Ben walked up to the glass window of the door, and they noticed him. One scientist walked up and shoved the curtain in front of his face to block his field of vision. The trio sat in silence.

"What the hell was that? We get pushed out of the way and get no answers?" Thomas exclaimed in a fit of frustration.

"The best we can do is wait until they get out, then we can see what's going on. We still don't even know the truth yet." Lincoln was interrupted by screaming coming from the hospital room. The group turned to stare at the door and heard constant outbursts such as "Hold him down!" and "Grab the sedative!"

"We should step away, guys," Lincoln said. They turned and walked away from the door. They returned to the sword and stood around it as if they were inspecting it.

The machines that it was connected to were starting to beep like crazy.

The glass of the dome surrounding the blade started to crack. Little by little, the glass was giving way. Before anyone could react, the glass exploded. The blast was so powerful that it threw the three men across the room, leaving black-and-blue bruises and blast marks.

The entire floor seemed to be demolished, as if a twister had roared through. Lincoln was buried in debris, and his face was covered in blood. He struggled to look up and saw none of his friends. He assumed that most of them were buried too far in the rubble. He looked at where the sword used to be and saw that there was a humanoid figure emerging from a blinding twirl of flashing light. The light slowly faded away like the wind, leaving a man standing in the middle of the wreckage. He looked around and smiled.

"Good to have my presence known," the intruder said.

He walked around the floor and noticed Thaw laying on the ground. Lincoln tried to shuffle out of his predicament. He tried to move, but it was futile. The weight of the debris was too great. The man's eyes glowed red, with nonexistent pupils. The antimatter ceiling lights reflected off of his metallic skin as he stood proud and with purpose. The red octagon emblazoned on his chest pulsated like a heartbeat.

He approached Thaw and bent down to his level.

"You are the reason why I'm like this," the man said with malice. "You don't know who I am, but I sure as hell know you, Lincoln Thaw." The man acted as if he was possessed.

"How do you know my name?" Lincoln asked.

"You seem to forget. My name is Raheem Gorroff. We've met before."

Lincoln's heart dropped, and he broke into a cold sweat.

"Thanks to Excalibur, my body is now at its peak. I can travel anywhere in the world in a matter of seconds. Nothing on this planet can stop me. I will eliminate you and your American friends one by one. I'll make you watch as I cut each of their throats wide open."

"Who are you? You're not human!" Lincoln responded.

"Oh, I am. I'm the most powerful human on the planet at the moment. And right now, you're the most vulnerable person. But sadly, I can't kill you right now." Raheem looked at the sword and smiled. "I have a promise to keep."

He picked up Excalibur. His smile was interrupted when he heard an alarm go off; security from the upper floors flooded the room and pointed pistols at him. He looked around and surveyed the armed guards. To him they were easy targets.

"Thirty against one. It hardly seems fair," he muttered while grasping Excalibur. The guards struggled to keep their composure and raised their guns. One guard had the courage to speak.

"You are trespassing on Roland Industries property!" he yelled. "Put your hands over your head and drop the sword immediately!"

"The only thing I'm surrounded by is dismay and men who are about to meet their maker," Raheem said. He disappeared in a flash of gold. Every guard stood his ground.

Suddenly, Raheem flashed back into existence right in front of one guard and slashed him with the sword, inflicting horrific gashes into his torso. He disappeared again and reappeared in front of two other guards, stabbing them simultaneously on the sharp blade. He yanked the sword from their bodies and disappeared again. The remaining officers shot at him with everything they had but couldn't land a single bullet on the mysterious infiltrator. He kept phasing in and out of view until every guard lay dead.

One final guard stood above the rest and inched his way toward the door. He took one step closer to the exit and kept his pistol out. His hands trembled, and his forehead dripped sweat. A moment later, and he turned to run.

A flash of gold appeared in front of him as Raheem pierced the sword straight through the guard's heart. He struggled for air and attempted to speak.

"W-Who are . . . you?" he asked, holding the blade lodged in his chest.

Raheem put his face closer to his and whispered.

"Consider me your Angel of Death. A Spector of Revenge. I am . . . the Golden Spector," he said, yanking Excalibur out of the guard's chest as his corpse fell to the ground with a thud.

"I can teleport anywhere I want in the vast quintiliverse and can kill twenty men with one hand. How about we test that theory out on Mr. Clinton?" the Spector said.

Lincoln shook with fear as he tried to move out of the debris in vain. He watched as Gorroff walked down the hallway and stopped right in front of the room where Clinton was being held. He heard screams and the breaking of bones. He closed his eyes to resist the images playing through his head of what was happening to the innocent people being slaughtered.

To Lincoln's horror, Clinton was thrown out of one of the tinted black windows and hit the ground on his back. Clinton's face met a steel box full of equipment that abruptly halted his slide across the floor. He spat out blood and attempted to reach his hand over the table next to him, the muscles on his arm shaking violently. He finally managed to pull himself over the table and took a deep breath. But before he had the chance to do anything else, he saw the golden flash of death shine in front of him. Gorroff punched him in the face so hard that it knocked him back to the floor. Then he stood over him triumphantly and took slow steps toward Clinton as the bruised and battered man tried to crawl away.

"It's a good feeling knowing I can finally finish you off," the Golden Spector said, placing the sword on the table that Clinton was leaning on. He picked Clinton up by his hair and slammed his face against the table three times. He threw him to the other side of the room, leaving a pool of blood on the table. Clinton's calm demeanor had vanished. His suit was shredded, and his face was covered in blood and sweat. His left eye twitched from the pain. The Spector smiled and walked toward him.

"When I'm done with you, you'll wish you were never born," he said. He stopped right in front of him and raised a foot to stomp on his face.

Without warning, he felt something impale his back. He stopped and turned around to see Lincoln holding Excalibur in his chest. Gorroff broke out in laughter and turned around, pushing him back. He calmly took out the sword out of his chest and looked at Lincoln.

"I was going to leave you off the hook, but I see you have a death wish. Let me honor that wish for you."

He swung the sword at him. Lincoln sprinted and looked for a weapon. He was used to being in combat, but fighting a man who could teleport was different. He grabbed one of the guns from the floor and cocked it. The Spector appeared right in front of him, and Thaw wasted no time pulling the trigger. The bullet pierced a vein in Gorroff's skin. The blood in his veins boiled with rage. He shot him a dark look that only a mad man could give once they had crossed over the limit. He faded out of existence and disappeared completely. Thaw looked around the room once more, awaiting his return. To his horror, he felt a rush of wind behind him, and he jerked his head around. Thaw's soul felt like it was being crushed at the horrific sight.

"I really didn't want to kill anybody today," the Spector said. "To be truthful, this has been an excellent warm-up for me. I thank you dearly for that."

He picked up Ben by the throat. Ben's feet didn't touch the ground at all. He could feel the air being forced out of his lungs. He held onto the Spector's hand to release it, but the grip only grew tighter. Thaw flung his arm up to shoot the Spector again, but Spector disappeared and reappeared on to the side of the room still holding Ben by his throat. With his other hand, he pulled out Excalibur and touched the tip of the blade to Ben's stomach. Ben's eyes radiated fear as he turned to Thaw, but all he could do was watch. It didn't matter what weapon he had. Nothing could prevent the inevitable.

He plunged the blade in Ben's stomach and deep into his spine. Ben screamed as he felt the blade split through him. Being the only human to ever enter the Multi-Precinct made Raheem even smarter and more precise when it came to fighting. Thaw roared with madness and despair as he ran at this diabolical man. He looked back at Ben and leaned in before dissipating away for the final time.

"Expect more pain from me, you cripple," he whispered and vanished, leaving Ben to drop to the floor.

Thaw ran up and cradled Ben in his arms. He desperately tried to help him up and was able to sit him down on a nearby chair. He heard footsteps from upstairs and turned to see a SWAT team invading the floor. Ben sobbed tears that mixed with the bloodstains on his shirt. He trembled as he spoke.

"L-Lincoln, I . . . can't feel my legs," he said.

Lincoln held Ben as tears of pain streamed down his face. He watched as the SWAT team engulfed the place and soon helped Ben get back to the upper levels of the building.

★ ★ ★

"In other news, a catastrophic event rocked the main Roland Industries headquarters in downtown Norfolk today. The culprit responsible for the attack on BULL was identified. The suspect's name is Raheem Gorroff. Officials have said to stay away if you see

him and to contact the federal government immediately. The death toll reached a total of thirty-eight, leaving only five injured but alive: Lincoln Thaw, Benjamin Frost, Thomas Lunardi, James Clinton, and Leonard Pascale. Benjamin Frost had only this to say . . . "

"*It was like seeing a Spector,*" said Ben on camera. "*A G-Golden Spector. If you see it, don't stop running!*"

The reporter reappeared onscreen.

"*The survivors are being treated. Whoever sees this mysterious 'Golden Spector' is advised to keep their distance and contact local authorities immediately. This is Dale Davison reporting to you live from News Channel 10.*"

Thomas turned off the set and threw the TV remote on the table next to his bed. The four men were all on hospital beds with IVs and heart monitors. The room was completely white with two beds near one side and the other two beds across from them. Their bodies ached, and their broken bones made the feeling even more excruciating. Lincoln was the luckiest out of the group: he was the least injured.

"So, his name is Raheem," Thomas said with malice.

"Apparently his name is the 'Golden Spector' now. Kind of suits him," Ben added. Thomas leaned in to get a better look.

"The next time I see him, he's gonna be a 'Dead Spector,'" Thomas added. He looked away and slithered back into his pillow.

"I know exactly who he was," Lincoln said.

"You better brief us, Thaw. We almost died because this guy was so pissed off," Ben said.

"It was the search-and-salvage mission from a few days ago when we almost killed the leader of the Souls of Death," Lincoln began.

"I thought you fried the son of a bitch!" Thomas said.

"Well, obviously we managed to piss off his son. Now he's out for revenge. How the hell he got to look like a ghost coming out of the grave, I don't know," Lincoln said.

Ben thought about the way he moved, acted, and most importantly, how he was able to pinpoint exactly where to stab him in the spine through his torso. Under normal circumstances, that puncture wound would've killed anybody. But he moved the blade expertly, avoiding any vital organs.

"How was he able to disappear and reappear so fast?" Ben asked.

"That's something that we have yet to find out," Lincoln said. "To be honest, we're facing the actual Excalibur and a terrorist with the ability to disappear. I guess the possibility of war is truly endless."

Thomas turned around and leaned in. His face was in pure shock.

"Wait, what the hell do you mean, Excalibur?" he asked.

"Ben and I think that the weapon that Raheem used is Excalibur," Lincoln said. Awkward silence filled the room. Ben and Lincoln knew Thomas was a skeptic about anything magical or paranormal. Thomas smiled weakly.

"Excalibur, huh? I bet the Easter Bunny and Santa Claus gave it to him," Thomas mocked.

Ben glared at him as he felt a surge of agony. He clutched the two protective bars on his hospital bed. His knuckles turned white and he spasmed uncontrollably. Lincoln and Thomas screamed for help.

A group of doctors heard the commotion and rushed in. They rolled Ben out of the room a moment later. Everyone else laid in silence in shock of what had happened. Suddenly, a familiar voice finally spoke up.

"What the hell was that?" Clinton asked.

"Welcome to the party, Sleeping Beauty," Thomas said. "Ben just had a major freak-out."

"You mean Benjamin Frost? He's dead to me anyway. I know exactly how his life is gonna turn out. He makes himself into something more than just human," Clinton said, laughing.

His laughter came to a screeching halt when he noticed Lincoln struggling to get out of bed. Lincoln could feel his bones cracking and popping as his bare feet touched the ground. The only thing that kept him alive was the rage coursing through his veins. He limped over to Clinton's bed. The blast temporarily sprained his arm and leg, but he was healing quite fast. His adrenaline temporarily eliminated his pain. When he finally reached Clinton's bed, he grabbed the safety bar and leaned in closely.

"Listen and listen well. I don't care that you're rich. I don't care that you have a multi-trillion-dollar job. I especially don't give a damn that you have associates everywhere at your disposal. But what I do care about is how people treat my friends. So if you ever talk like that about Ben again, I'll make sure you don't end up in a hospital. You'll be in a morgue. Do I make myself clear?"

"Yes, sir," Clinton said.

"That's what I thought." Lincoln felt his leg trembling. He limped back to his bed, face twisted into a scowl. He laid back on his bed and winced in pain until the relief hit him.

Wherever this man was—this Golden Spector—he would pay dearly for his deadly actions. Lincoln wouldn't rest until he made damn sure that every last little thing that he did would come back around and get him. In Thaw's eyes, everything came full circle. Raheem Gorroff would pay dearly for his actions. Evil came in all shapes and sizes; but it had to be stopped.

Thaw closed his eyes and inhaled. He felt the oxygen overtake his lungs. Suddenly, his thoughts were interrupted.

"Hey, Thaw, you okay over there?" Thomas asked.

"I'm fine. But the Spector made one crucial mistake," Lincoln responded.

Thomas raised an eyebrow. "What's that, bub?"

"He left us alive."

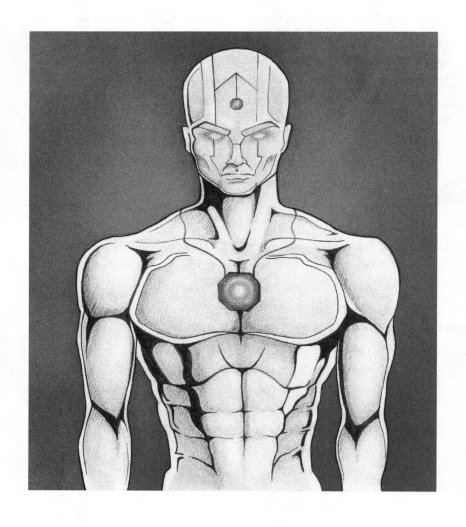

CHAPTER 6

TWO WEEKS LATER, THE WORLD was under siege from the Golden Spector and consumed by a state of mass panic. The president was placed under constant supervision by the Secret Service, and the White House was under lockdown.

The Spector appeared in places all around the world, targeting the men and women responsible for the mission that nearly killed his father. Some citizens remained in denial, unable to believe in what seemed like science fiction nonsense. Half the team that helped with the mission had already been murdered; as a safety precaution, Lincoln, Thomas, and Clinton were placed in solitary confinement. Everyone knew that wasn't going to be enough to stop the Spector, but they were willing to try anything.

Ben's spinal cord was infected and the doctors at Roland Industries speculated that it had been injected with a chemical compound that attacked his muscle tissue, but the substance itself remained unidentified. Ben was given a strong sleeping agent called *TQR-8* that slowed the heart rate down eight times the normal speed, leaving the subject unconscious so that the muscles and other body systems could easily undergo operation. Ben would be in a coma until further notice.

Meanwhile, Lincoln, Thomas, and Clinton were losing their minds in the cement confines of their temporary prisons. Lincoln tried to calm everyone down, seeking to instill positivity. Clinton remained highly reserved to avoid being emotionally compromised. Thomas and Clinton were now getting into petty arguments with one another.

"Listen, if we continue to act like children, we'll get nowhere," Lincoln said. He turned to face Clinton.

"Is there anything we can use to fight Raheem? I know you know there are machines that Roland Industries has developed in the past that may help us."

"We have a weapon called the Particle Solidifier," he said. "It basically makes any and all particles floating in the air around us stop instantaneously, no matter where they are. Even particles moving at the speed of sound could be stopped at the exact moment we wanted. The Australians developed it and sold us the blueprints. Only two prototypes have ever been successfully made."

"Remind me, please, why the military hasn't used that yet?" Thomas asked.

"Because idiots like you would end up abusing it. It was exclusively designed for combat, but one volunteer ended up ripping apart the particles in his body on the molecular level. You'd be dead instantly," Clinton said.

"Where can we find them?" Thomas asked.

"One's in Australia, the other in Virginia Beach. It's sealed in a bunker near Norfolk, underground."

"All we have to do is get there," Thomas said.

"How about we wait until the next guard comes around and we can thump 'em?" Thomas recommended.

Clinton and Thaw gave him a skeptical look.

"Were you dropped on your head when you were a kid?" Clinton asked. "Or are you just naturally this dumb?"

"Actually, I almost was, but my mom caught me at the last minute, jackass," Thomas retorted.

Suddenly, Lincoln leaned over and smacked Clinton upside the head. He gave Thaw a nasty look and glared at the ground to cover his embarrassment. Thaw just leaned over and shot Thomas an angry look.

***

In Washington, DC, the president was on a call with the supervisor of HAS, or the Human Advancement Station, in the secret bunker located beneath downtown Norfolk.

The head scientist in charge of HAS, Adam Braxton, stood with his cell phone pressed against his ear. He was discussing every weapon in their arsenal that could potentially be used to neutralize this international threat. HAS was funded by Roland Industries, and ever since the company started to successfully sponsor his secret corporation, he took every chance he got to invent something beneficial to society.

"Sir, the Particle Solidifier is the only line of defense for this guy. It's the only weapon that can possibly do anything to counteract him," Adam said.

"Adam, we need every weapon we can get," the president said. *"I don't care if they're in their prototype stage. I don't care if they're not done being built. We need to protect the American people effective immediately."*

Adam sighed and pictured the weapon he was dreading to bring up.

"There's one weapon that's been sealed behind glass for some time. My team and I were developing it back in 2006 and terminated the project because we didn't find any volunteers to test its agility. None of the volunteers were physically fit to wear it."

"Anything helps. What is it?"

"Sir, it's a full-body modifier. Roland Industries wanted to help our boys over in Afghanistan, so we pitched an idea of a particle-enhanced, sense-multiplying, strength accumulator. It's made out of a flexible bulletproof fabric cut from Chobham armor. The armor tanks use that stuff. We infused it with a molecular-healing epidermis to prevent the wearer from being hurt."

"Son, I didn't ask for a school lesson. Can we bring the project back online, yes or no?"

"Theoretically, sir, yes. But we'd need someone to be in the suit to test all its functions."

"There's a man who's a victim of the Golden Spector. He's currently in solitary confinement for protection, but I think he'd be more than qualified to test your little project."

"Sir, please elaborate. I don't want some random guy in a multi-billion-dollar suit."

"His name's Thomas Lunardi."

"Sir, if he's in solitary confinement, there's a reason. I don't want some jarhead taking over my project. It'll create a bad reputation for me and the company."

"If you're not pleased with him, there is another officer on their team. Their sniper, Lincoln Thaw. If you'd prefer someone with a sharp eye, I'd go with him. He's the most qualified, physically fit, and he's performed well." The president hung up.

"Mr. President? Mr. President?" Adam asked, but there was no response. He put his phone down and closed his eyes in frustration. He turned to face the wall behind his desk and leaned back. He admired the uncompleted prototype of the suit that stood poised and dormant behind glass. It was statuesque, with its arms and legs fixed in position. The suit was mostly black, with navy blue armored plates. One arm had a blade in a holster that was black as well to seem almost camouflaged in the suit. The mask was a very simple design: all black, with two holes for a wider field of vision.

"I guess it's finally time for you to show your true colors, huh?" Adam asked aloud. He turned around and reached in his drawer to pull out a file. He gazed at the blueprints that the Australians had given him. In the fine print, he noticed the bottom of the document:

Weapon size can be altered with any function of mechanics. By order 745, this foreign weapon can be changed in any way the receiver sees fit.

He glanced back at the suit and quickly picked up his cell phone. He dialed one of his scientific associates named Kayla Mersey. A moment later, he heard her familiar voice.

"What is it, Adam?" she asked.

"Tell the president we're going to have the best of both worlds! The Body Modifier and the Particle Solidifier are going to be one unit," Adam said.

"What are you saying?" she asked.

"We're going to make the Solidifier smaller and put it on the suit. If this works, America may stand a chance."

There was a long silence. No one had mentioned this idea before. Seconds seemed like hours in anticipation of her response.

"Adam, I want you to transport the suit to Sector Twelve along with the plans for the Solidifier. I want any and all plans for both weapons. Schematics, equipment, hell, even trial videos that we've made on them in the past."

"Ma'am, you'll have everything in less than an hour."

"Good work, Adam," she said before hanging up. Adam sat down and started to assemble his plans.

Aura floated in the Multi-Precinct. She reached out her arms to connect herself to the billions of Earths displayed before her. Her eyes were closed, concentrating and channeling her own life force into the infinite abyss. A strobing light broke her concentration a moment later. She opened her eyes to see Raheem hovering near her and wearing a sinister smile.

"I see you have discovered a gateway to the Multi-Precinct. Your abilities grow stronger."

"Do you know how many people I've killed? How much vengeance

I've delivered?" he asked while his skin turned to its golden state of terror.

"You have executed a maximum of forty-six people within the United States of America, leading to a mass panic."

"So, you've been keeping up with me, huh? You think that you spying on me is supposed to intimidate me? It does quite the opposite. I've—"

"Your childish antics have proven you are unfit to have the abilities you have been gifted, as I have stated before. You are no more of a threat to me than the world's most terrifying ant. Your repeated attempts to intimidate me are futile and ill-timed. Your alias name, the Golden Spector, will eventually lead to your death if you continue down this path of self-destruction."

"When the world hears the name Golden Spector, they will fall to their knees in terror. I will rule the world with an iron fist. My power is without limits and without adversary." He grasped Excalibur tightly in his hand.

"You're mistaken. Given time and patience, a worthy adversary will soon arise to defeat you against unfathomable odds. You two will fight until one falls."

"Unless that person wants to die, I don't think I'll ever fight a worthy adversary. My power is too great."

"I recommend that you watch your back. Because at any moment, your throne of power will be obliterated by this individual." Aura turned her back to Raheem. She spread her arms out again, attempting to reconnect with the multiverse.

Raheem knew deep in his heart that Aura was right. He noticed his arms were reverting back to their original color against his will. His whole body suddenly reformed back to its human state. Raheem grew angry at his sudden vulnerability.

"Wait, what's happening?" he screamed as his body reverted to its original form.

"The angrier you feel, the less power you have. Your time here will be over in a matter of seconds. No ordinary human can withstand being here with me very long. Goodbye, Mr. Gorroff."

In that moment, Raheem faded out of existence and returned abruptly to Earth. The next thing he knew, he was teleported, falling to the sand of Iraq. He crash-landed in the smoldering hot sand and screamed in agony as he hit the grainy surface of the desert. He winced as he took a few steps struggling to get up. He turned and looked up, screaming as Excalibur came hurling down and landed parallel to his head.

With the intent of defying Aura, he attempted to change into his golden form. However, he could not. He focused again, but to no avail. As far as he was concerned, he was in the middle of nowhere. He had to teleport to get back to his people.

If he was going to stay in the golden superhuman form he so craved, he had to stay self-confident without doubt or insecurity. He sluggishly got up under the harsh sun. His eyelids dilated so quickly that he had to shield his eyes. The sand felt strangely alien beneath his feet. He had teleported so many times that he had forgotten the feeling of being on regular ground. He had to find the man who wounded his father somehow or at the very least get revenge by wiping out all who could have been involved. He loved the feeling of being at a destination in a matter of a second. He scanned his environment and saw nothing but sand. He was nowhere near his home. He knew what he had to do. He closed his eyes and concentrated.

"On the count of three," he whispered softly.

"One . . . " he said as he tried to connect to his inner being. He remembered how he felt as the Golden Spector and tried to reconnect with that rare feeling of sadistic control.

"Two . . . " He remembered how he crippled Clinton, murdered forty-six people, stole Excalibur, and disabled Ben. He smiled as he felt his power returning.

"Three . . . " he said as his body morphed back into its Spector form. He didn't feel pain anymore. No more burning in the veins, no more peeling of his torched skin. He had come to hate his regular human self. He was weak as a regular human. But in this advanced form, he was unstoppable. He looked at his body and grinned even more when he saw the golden sword shining bright in the sand. He leaned down and grabbed it. He looked into the distance, thought carefully, and teleported away, leaving a curl of sand in his wake.

★★★

He arrived in The Village, which had been recently bombarded by terrorists. Souls of Death activists swarmed the village because word had spread that the Golden Spector first appeared there. They wanted to work with the Spector so they could wipe out any and all foes.

Hakim Gorroff lay in his bed, his face crusted in blood. His vision was still blurry from the explosion, and the heat didn't help matters. All of his limbs ached. He knew about what happened to his son. He simply couldn't get up in his condition. Suddenly, a bright flash of twirling gold light appeared somewhere near the center of the village, whipping wind and sand everywhere. Raheem stepped out of the light a moment later and looked around as it faded.

The villagers and activists stared in amazement. Raheem stared back at them with his red, piercing eyes and a sinister smile.

"Father, I'm home," Raheem said.

The ground below his feet turned to gold as he walked forward. The people backed away slowly as he marched through the throngs to find his father. He entered the tent. A medic sitting next to his bed turned to face Raheem in shock.

"Get out," Raheem commanded.

The doctor immediately fled the tent. Raheem walked to the chair and sat down, facing his father. He watched his dad shift in bed and slowly raise his eyelids. Hakim nearly fell out of bed when he recognized his son. Raheem clenched his fist, and a golden barrier materialized on the side of the bed, preventing him from falling.

"Raheem, what the hell happened to you?" Hakim asked. "Who did this?" He leaned over and put both hands on Raheem's cheeks.

Raheem touched his father's hands, and his sinister smile turned to a comforting grin.

"It's okay, Father," Raheem said. "I took care of him and all the people responsible."

"You hurt them?" he asked.

"Yes, Father."

"Good. The less people that we have to worry about, the better."

"Father, I've seen things. Things that no mere mortal such as ourselves have ever witnessed. There are other Earths. Parallel places that have different outcomes, different meanings, and different scenarios."

"Son, you can tell me all about other places later. But do you have it?"

Raheem reached down and gently placed Excalibur on his bed. The sheets scrunched from the weight of the magnificent, ancient weapon.

Hakim stared at it and laughed. He put one hand on the handle and the other below the blade. He lifted it and noticed that it was heavier than expected. His muscles were fatigued, and his arms trembled uncontrollably. He marveled at this golden piece of artwork, but his eyes were drawn to his own reflection.

He noticed that the handle of the sword started to feel hotter. He tried to rip his hand away, but some mysterious force led his hand to grip the handle tighter.

He started to panic.

"Raheem, get this thing off of me. Do it now!" Raheem clutched the handle of the blade. He tried to yank the sword away, but it reacted to his attempt. He was thrown across the tent and out beyond the tarp that protected patients from the harsh sun. He tried to run back in but was abruptly halted by an invisible force.

Raheem tried to teleport through but was thrown down into the sand. Hakim's arm was engulfed with the same golden light that took over Raheem's body. The light didn't stop until his whole form was completely immersed in it. Raheem pounded on the force field with his fists and stopped when his father's screams suddenly ceased.

The force field suddenly dissipated. The sword flew out of the cot, slicing through the thick canvas like tissue paper. It landed blade first on the sand at Raheem's feet.

There Hakim stood. The battle scar on his face had disappeared and healed. His age was fifty-nine, but now he looked as if he were twenty-six. His hair was shorter, and the silver strands were replaced by jet black. There was no indication that he had ever been in an accident. Hakim stepped into the sunlight and closed his eyes. Raheem and the rest of the soldiers watched in disbelief. Some people had their weapons ready in case something sinister happened. But they were scared. They had no idea what was going on or what was happening.

"F-Father?" Raheem stuttered. The golden aura inside him dissipated due to this surge of fear and concern. Hakim looked at him and smiled the most genuine, happy smile that Raheem ever saw from him. He walked up to Raheem and firmly gripped his shoulders.

"Son, I couldn't be better. I haven't felt this alive in years," Hakim said, laughing.

Suddenly, one of the nervous villagers accidently fired his weapon. The bullets hit Hakim's back but simply rebounded. He winced in pain.

Raheem snapped his head back and screamed, "Hold your fire!" Hakim stepped back and walked toward the man who pulled the trigger. He casually walked over to him and smiled. The man was in sheer terror.

"S-Sir, I'm so sorry. I didn't mean to . . . " he blurted out.

"You're fine. It's okay," he said as he clenched his fist. In one swift unsuspecting motion, he swung his fist up and punched the man so hard that he flew into the air and hurled down into the sand, snapping his arm on impact. He turned around and stretched his fingers.

"Oh, Raheem, you think you're the only one that was gifted?" Hakim asked. He turned to the people crowding the area and walked to them. They backed away quickly in fear.

"Listen up, we're going to take America by storm. How many of you have lost loved ones or have ever wanted to take revenge upon the people that have infiltrated your village and raided your homes?" Hakim asked. The crowd erupted in a frenzy. "How many of you are sick and tired of living in fear of what the Americans will do next?" The crowd loved him. They seemed to glow with hope. They admired him like a god, not even questioning what had happened to him. They only cared about having a firm leader to achieve victory over the US. "The United States of America will be our new fighting grounds! We will train! We will fight! We will be avenged my brothers!" The crowd erupted, uncontrollable. If Hakim said to do something, they would do anything. Hakim and Raheem stood next to each other and watched as their Iraqi kingdom screamed and yelled in support.

"Lincoln Thaw has no idea what is coming to him," Raheem said.

CHAPTER 7

"DADDY? ARE YOU AWAKE?" THEIA asked with tears streaming down her face. Benjamin was in the hospital with IV lines pouring out of machines. His kids were on either side of his bed, watching their father's face intently, waiting and hoping for him to wake up and smile.

"Daddy, please wake up. We need you. I love you," his son Zachary said. His tear-filled eyes were red, making his vision blurry. Veronica stood close to Zachary, fighting the urge to cry. Her eyes revealed heartache and concern.

She turned to her husband as he lay unconscious.

"Honey, it's me. You may not be able to hear me, but if you can, please. Your family misses you. I miss you. All those years in the military made you strong." She stepped closer to his bed, her eyes unwavering from his badly bruised face. A trail of dried blood curved around his right eye and to his mouth. There was a dried blood on his lip. He was hooked up to telemetric equipment. His spine had been severed in two places and the doctors said it was doubtful he would walk again.

"I know you can pull through. I don't care if you're in a wheelchair.

I don't care if you won't physically be the same. I want my Ben back. I want my husband," she sobbed. "You helped me get through a tough part in my life when not many people could help. My family scolded me while you held my hand and guided me through the dark. You helped Lincoln cope with the loss of his daughter when she was kidnapped. That was the sweetest, most selfless thing I have seen anyone do. Lincoln was still struggling, and pretty soon we grew closer until he became a part of our family." She sniffled and wiped away her tears.

"Please come back to me. I love you, Benjamin Frost," she said. She closed her green eyes and leaned in to kiss her husband.

★ ★ ★

In Norfolk, the secret bunker was ready for its first test run for the body enhancer in years. Lincoln stood in a middle of a pure white room with a metallic silver floor. The room seemed to stretch forever.

Lincoln looked down, admiring his armored suit. It had been molded to fit his physique. The suit's blue armored plates made him appear more menacing than ever. He shook his arms and stretched his legs. He found the suit strangely liberating. He always sought to be the strongest soldier, but now he could feel that this suit had granted him this wish. He moved his left arm to his face and studied the peculiar device strapped to his wrist. It was the size of a wristwatch, with a firm, elastic band. The main parts of the suit had green with blue wires interloping in and out of the outer levels to the inner mechanics. It hummed quietly, with heat emanating onto his skin. It felt alive. He lifted his other arm and tapped his Bluetooth earpiece to talk.

"So this is a Particle Solidifier?" Lincoln asked.

"*It's an aerodynamic inner molecular inhibitor,*" Adam said.

"In English, please," Lincoln said.

"*Once you activate the device on your arm, it will restrict all the particles in the air, immobilizing your enemy.*"

"Good enough for me."

"*Remember, this is just a training course to see how you act and react with the suit. Nothing more and nothing less. If you need us to stop, all you have to do is say so."*

Adam was in the control room, beneath the white bunker-like space where Lincoln stood. Everywhere around Adam, there were flashing controls, dials, knobs, and keyboards. Thomas sat next to him in a rolling chair, admiring Adam's equipment. He reached out his hand to press a flashing light, but Adam quickly smacked it.

"I just wanted to touch it," Thomas said.

"All right, Thaw. Are you ready?" Adam asked. He watched Lincoln through a bank of monitors, the cameras of which surrounded Lincoln in the bunker. Lincoln took a deep breath and looked intently at a camera that was bolted to the ceiling.

"I'm ready," he said with confidence.

Adam leaned back and flipped a large red switch to the right of the control panel in front of him. An automated voice spoke through overhead speakers.

"Welcome. This field test will test your agility, strength, and reaction time," said a female British voice. *"Please feel free to use any weapons at your disposal. HAS is not responsible for death, injury, brain trauma, puncture wounds, infectious injections, and permanent scars. Remember, this test only lasts for three minutes. The highest you can score is a 100 percent. Good luck and thank you for using HAS, human advancement at its finest. Your test will now begin."*

"Oh, is that all?" Lincoln joked.

The whole room changed in a matter of seconds.

"You might want to put on your mask," Adam said. Lincoln reached into his back pocket and quickly put on the black mask. He couldn't see anything until a tiny white ball of light emerged and quickly engulfed his vision. He tried shaking his head, but he was momentarily blinded. But within an instant, he could see everything clearly.

"Good evening, user," said the voice. *"You have approximately three minutes to complete your task. Right now, Mr. Braxton has put you in the middle of the African jungle."*

"On safari? Oh, sure, that makes sense," Lincoln said, squinting to adjust to his surroundings. The artificial sun shined high above in the sky. He was suddenly standing on a silver platform that stretched a mile across. The oval was so abstract in the middle of the jungle. He was in a wide-open space so anything could come out and attack at any given moment. He could hear monkeys shrieking and lions roaring in the distance. He heard the sound of leaves rustling in the baobab trees. Crickets chirped in every direction.

"This is amazing," he stuttered in awe. "I didn't know that this kind of tech was even possible."

In the control room below, Adam smirked and flipped a switch. Lincoln was still looking around him, wondering what was going to happen next, when a familiar voice snapped him back to reality.

"Mr. Thaw, I detect something strong on my thermal radar. I advise you use caution. When the opponent reaches you, I will be out of contact to allow you to engage however you please."

Lincoln stood in silence. Suddenly, he felt the ground shake. His heart raced. The ground around him rumbled.

THUD!

The voice in his ear returned. *"Mr. Thaw, I wish you the best of luck. Remember this crucial detail: nothing is real, and you can stop the simulation by speaking out."*

The ground shook again, and Lincoln grew uneasy. The birds in the distant trees all flew away at once. He saw the silhouette now. It was that of a humanoid figure emerging from the shade of a copse of trees.

Thud! The figure stood at the tree line, the very edge of light and shadow. Lincoln felt tension in the air and instantly knew he was the target. It was a massive figure, standing maybe nine or ten feet tall, but with the eyes of a human.

It can't be. There's no way a human can be that size, Lincoln thought. A moment later, he saw fur on the humanoid's arms and legs. It all became horrifically clear.

The creature walked out of the shade slowly. Its fur was a tawny orange with terrifying, protruding muscles. Its head was enormous, with its nose pushed in and flaring nostrils for easier inhalation. Lincoln focused on its eyes. They were a dark brown color that surrounded deep black pupils. This creature was truly a sight, but it was about to be the last sight he would ever see in this virtual world if he didn't concentrate. The great beast turned and roared in anger.

"Meet the Gigantopithecus," Adam said in Lincoln's earpiece, snapping him back to reality. He struggled to his feet. *"It went extinct about a nine million years ago, give or take a hundred thousand years."*

"He can't handle this," Thomas said. "He fights real people, not animals that have been extinct for millions of years. You serious?"

"I assure you this is only a simulation," Adam said. "It's being conducted to see if he's fit to wear the suit. I simply require knowledge on how he is going to kill the beast. Absolutely none of what he sees is real."

"Yeah, you're gonna kill him when you get your answer," Thomas said.

In the simulation, Lincoln faced this formidable challenge. The great ape stepped onto the opposite side of the platform and glared at him.

"Okay, King Kong. It's you and me, baby," Lincoln said.

The Gigantopithecus roared once more and started to charge on all fours. Lincoln closed his eyes and shot them back open in concentration. He reached into his leg pouch and pulled out a grappling gun. He whipped the gun around and shot a distant tree. The hook rocketed through the air.

As the ape rushed closer, Lincoln pressed the button and zipped out of the way fast enough that the ape crashed into a tree head-first. Lincoln landed on the tree branch that he shot and leaned on it, squatting. He quickly recoiled the rope back into the grappling gun and looked up to see where the creature was. He didn't see anything. The field was empty and unsettlingly quiet. He suddenly felt a force grabbing his back and ribs. The force squeezed tightly and tossed him into the field. He struggled to get up. His arms had been badly bruised. The armor of his suit had been slashed at the arms, revealing road rash. To his amazement, he watched as his skin started to heal. A moment later, the lining of the suit did as well.

The ape charged at him again, but this time he was ready. The ape jumped into the air and Lincoln reached into his shoulder pouch and whipped out a .45-caliber with a dual-action silencer. Without thinking, he pulled the trigger three times. The ape closed its mouth quickly and tried to claw at him, but he back flipped and landed on his feet. The creature roared in agony and writhed on the ground.

"Did I just do that?!" he yelled.

The creature roared to life a moment later, slapping him in the face with a giant hand. He flew backward into a tree, breaking it on impact. His spine shook violently before he rose to his feet. He felt rage surge inside and knew at once that he was out for blood. Simulation or no simulation, this ape was going down.

He sprinted faster than he ever had before. Holding the .45 in his left hand, he reached his right hand for his blade. He jumped from the ground and landed on the creature's face. He propelled himself into the air. Once he was high enough, he turned and flung the blade at the Gigantopithecus's eye. It roared once more, and Lincoln fired the .45 into his other eye. The giant ape fell back to earth. Once the creature was completely sightless, Lincoln landed, reached into his leg pocket, and pulled out a small white metal ball the size of a marble. It had a silvery metal ring around it to contain the deadly substance within. One small red button was visible on the side. He flicked the button, causing it to strobe in a bright flash.

"The bigger you are, the harder you fall," he said as he threw it at the creature. It detonated right in the ape's face, causing a white smoky substance to spill all over its mouth and nose, morphing solidly against its skin. The creature tried to rip the substance off, but to no avail. The more it swung around, the more energy it burned and air it wasted. It soon suffocated and fell to the ground with a thud.

Lincoln put the .45 back in his arm holster and put the blade in the other arm holster. He looked up to the sky and threw out his arms.

"I did it!" he yelled with a smile plastered on his face. He scanned his surroundings as they faded from view. Everything turned back into the familiar room from before. Once the jungle evaporated into nothing, he saw Thomas and Adam standing in front of him. Adam held a piece of paper and handed it to him. Lincoln took the paper and looked at Thomas in confusion. He read the paper in shock.

H.A.S
(Human Advancement Station)

— *Subject Name: Lincoln Thaw*
— *Reason for Test: Body Modifier Mk.1*
— *Subject Condition: Excellent*
— *Pass: Yes*
— *Score: 98%*

"I passed?" Lincoln asked.

"Indeed, you did," Adam said. "You're the only person to successfully use the modifier to its full potential."

"But why 98 percent? I'm not complaining or anything. I'm just curious."

"You focused a little too much on your surroundings rather than your opponent."

"Look, when you're in the military long enough, you learn your surroundings mean everything. If that beast was coming after me, I could hide or use my grappling gun to hook onto something and get away. If I may be so bold, I don't think you know too much about that aspect of combat."

"Yes, maybe you're right," Adam said, sighing. "I sometimes forget what other people think and experience. I'm sorry, but I didn't come up with the score. The simulation AI did."

"Error in simulation score. Recalculating now," said the female British voice from the AI intercom. Adam ran over to the computer to see the new score. He froze for a moment before turning to face Lincoln. He printed the new report and brought it to Lincoln. He handed him the new slip of paper, which read 100 percent.

"Well, Mr. Thaw. It looks like you were right and I was wrong. And you're the first person to ever outsmart the simulation as well. Didn't even think that was possible." Adam raised an eyebrow. "Mr. Thaw, do you mind removing your mask?"

"I like it on," Lincoln said. "Makes me feel powerful."

"With all due respect, Mr. Braxton, I believe Lincoln's had enough for one day," Thomas said, winking at Lincoln. "I think he wants to take a breather."

"Yeah, I think I'm going to lie down for a little bit and rest," Lincoln said, nodding at Thomas.

"All right, then. That's fine. You gentlemen go take your breather for now," Adam said. "I'm going to run the specs on the suit and see what advancements I can make. I noticed that your movements may have de-calibrated your weapons package. Please leave the suit in my workshop on my desk."

Lincoln nodded as Adam left the room. Once the door was closed, Thomas turned around and looked Lincoln up and down.

"Damn, that's the coolest thing I've ever seen," he said, admiring the design of the suit.

CHAPTER 8

IRAQ WAS SLOWLY BECOMING AN empire ruled by father and son. Baghdad was slowly rising to power and intimidating neighboring countries: Saudi Arabia, Syria, Kuwait, Iran, and Turkey. The whole world was frightened by this unnatural rise in exceptional power. Thousands of soldiers from the US's numerous allied powers flew in and attempted to infiltrate the newly empowered Iraq, but to no avail. They were slaughtered one by one. Iraqi operatives captured them, lined them on an execution wall, and fired away. They filmed it to intimidate and stop them.

Hakim and Raheem possessed evil, insidious power that no one could have imagined. Hakim was slowly starting to forget that he had grown younger. He truly believed he had not yet reached age fifty-six. Raheem noticed that his father was slowly growing more sinister than he ever had been. He always assisted his father no matter what situation they were overtaking. However, Hakim was overruling Raheem with each and every decision.

Raheem grew tired of it and threatened to leave Iraq; his father banished him and kept the sword as a trophy. In a fit of rage, Raheem traveled the world to do the only thing he had always known to do: find James Clinton. To the world, he had vanished the moment he left the hospital. Raheem tried looking for any trace of Clinton, but to no avail. It was as if he never existed.

Raheem tracked down and tortured many operatives who had been connected to Clinton, but they all said that he disappeared without a trace. He investigated further, traveling through Europe and Asia, teleporting everywhere, but he had no choice but to surrender.

He thought he knew the world like the back of his hand. He was angry with his father. Why would he do this to him? After searching the globe for Clinton, this was the thanks he got? So many questions rushed through his head as he sat in silence.

After hours in solitude, his eyes shot open at the realization of a grand master plan. *What if I steal the sword back from my father then ask Aura to show me an Earth where I win over my father and finally take Iraq back?* It was the perfect plan.

Convincing Aura to show him an Earth where he won would be the only issue.

In the Norfolk bunker, Adam sat at his computer running thousands of diagnostic tests from the simulation and analyzing different fight patterns and algorithms. As he watched the blue holographic screen flashing data, he pondered their situation. He developed this suit years ago when it was just a farfetched schematic that he left in the development stages for so long that he almost forgot about it. Disregarded by his superiors, he tossed the idea aside behind glass for years collecting dust, and here he was running tests on the nearly perfected prototype.

All his life, Adam pushed himself to emulate his role models, but mediocrity was the only thing that he felt. He surrounded himself in work to forget that melancholy fact.

"Computer, find Lincoln and Thomas, please," he asked.

A holographic projection showed him the two men. They were

talking alone in the trial simulation room. That room consisted of only white walls and thousands of tiles that activated in the holographic simulation process.

"When I was fighting that ape, it felt like all my muscles were turned to stone. Damn, that felt good. My senses were at an all-time high, and my brain felt like it was operating at one 100 percent. That suit is unlike anything I've ever felt before. It's like it was alive or something."

"Buddy, if you're gonna save the world, I think you need an overhaul with that thing. Besides, you need to rely on your experience over the fancy electronics that thing is littered with."

"Who the hell said I was gonna save the world?" Lincoln asked, still laughing with Thomas. But Thomas froze and shook his head, suddenly struck by the gravity of the moment.

"No way," he said, grabbing Lincoln by the shoulder. *"You're Lincoln Thaw, the man who can do anything. I've known you since boot camp, and even then, you always pushed yourself to the max and never looked back. Your daughter would've been proud of you. She looked up to you. Don't stop now."*

"I just wished I could've been able to save her from that . . . thing. If I actually saved her, then she could've seen all this."

"There's nothing you could've done. There are some things in this world we just can't change. If we let these things get the better of us, they'll eat us alive. To be honest, I was jealous of you sometimes."

"Really, man?" Lincoln asked.

"Damn right," Thomas said.

Adam only knew the two men for a short amount of time, but he was beginning to understand Lincoln, based on past experience. He lowered his head and let the sound of the computer hum its familiar tune of electronic engineering. He knew that from hearing this small piece of Lincoln's past, they had to win. Not only for the world, but also for Lincoln's daughter.

"Internal Bio-Schematics Rendering Process Completed," said the computerized voice. Adam returned to his work.

★ ★ ★

Thomas returned back home due to extreme fatigue, and Lincoln headed to the hospital to console Ben's family. He rushed through the doors and took the elevator upstairs to the third floor. He walked briskly to his left down the long hallway. Each room was big enough to fit at least three patients. He held daisies as a token attempt at normalcy: he figured his friend would appreciate a bouquet of flowers.

He stopped mid-way down the hallway and turned to Room 555. He leaned on the doorframe and lightly knocked on the door. He waited until he heard a faint, "Come in," from the other side. He opened the door and noticed that only Veronica was sitting at Ben's bedside.

"Where are the kids?" Lincoln asked. Veronica looked up to face him.

"At home with the babysitter," she said. "I wasn't going have them here day in and day out. They have school. Plus, I don't want them seeing their mommy crying."

"Good call. I was getting worried about them, too." Lincoln placed the daisies on the nightstand next to the telemetric equipment. "You know, I was hoping he would be—"

At that moment, Veronica got up from her chair, ran to him, and embraced him. She wrapped her arms around him, hugging him. Lincoln was thrown off guard but slowly hugged her back.

"The doctor said that he would be . . . " She paused between sobs. " . . . paralyzed from the waist down. The blast shook his spinal cord and broke his fourth and fifth vertebrae." Tears streamed down her face and dropped onto his jacket. Lincoln looked out the window, and his heart sank. He watched the sunlight pour through the window and onto the floor, filling the room with a golden color like some twisted omen.

"Veronica, I promise you. The man who did this to him will pay dearly for his sins. Not only for Ben, but for the countless other people he's murdered along the way."

"I'm sorry, Lincoln. But I think this may be out of your league."

Lincoln shifted his hands to her shoulders and moved her away from him to look into her eyes.

"Listen to me, Veronica. I've been in this business for nearly nineteen years, and believe me, I've almost given up multiple times. I know the feeling of hopelessness, fear, like you might never feel the same ever again. It gets better, believe me. I almost didn't believe that at first, either." He wiped away a tear from her face and stepped to the window, looking out over the sunlit city.

Veronica wiped away more tears and stared at him as he leaned on the windowsill. He looked like he was searching for something.

"What do you mean, didn't believe it at first?" she asked.

There was a long pause. Silence filled the room as Lincoln prepared himself to pour his heart out to answer her question. He closed his eyes and remembered his past. He didn't even bother turning around. He looked outward to the city.

"When I first joined the Marines, I always looked after my wife whenever I could. She had Stage IV lung cancer. Deep down, I denied the fact that she was inevitably going to pass away. God, I miss her voice so much. She was my calm in the storm. She had the key to my heart. Then she gave me news that rocked me to my core. She was pregnant.

"I thought she was going crazy," he continued. "I tried to explain that she was delusional. But she had me take her to the doctor; he confirmed it. She was just two months along. She held on as long as she could. She was always a great fighter. I felt terrible that I was being deployed again, and as soon as I came back exactly seven months later, I immediately went to the hospital to see her. When I came back, she was frail and weak. She wasn't herself. The light in her eyes that I had loved so much was fading away. I remember holding her hand—"

Tears made his vision blurry. Veronica put her hand over her mouth in shock. She had never heard the full story of Lincoln's wife.

"What did she say?" she asked

"I held her hand, and she said we had a baby girl. I was so thrilled. I promised her I'd quit the Marines and raise the child without any distractions. She had already named the child after her mother. Patricia. Patricia Cretella Thaw. I still remember promising her that I would protect her no matter what. She flat-lined in my arms just a few moments later, and I kissed her before they covered her face with the blanket. What happened next haunted me for years." Lincoln walked over to the same chair that Veronica sat on by Ben's bedside.

"You don't have to say it if you don't want to," Veronica said.

"It's fine. I'm used to the feeling by now. She was four years old, and I was in the kitchen cooking dinner while she was in the living room playing with her toys and watching TV. I loved her more than anyone could ever love anything. Suddenly, the power went out, and a blinding light flashed inside the house. I heard my daughter scream. I ran into the living room, grabbed her, and ran out of the house to the car. The fear we experienced when we got out was indescribable.

"A swirling white vortex was sucking in everything. The force was too strong, and I held onto a nearby tree. She held onto me for dear life. We lived on a ranch far away from anyone else. No one could hear us.

"At one point, she slipped out of my grasp. She was dangling in mid-air, about to be sucked into that damn thing. I will never forget her screams. She called out to me, but her grasp slipped, and she was sucked into the vortex. Seconds later, it went away without a trace. She was gone forever.

"I loathed myself for years. I turned to drinking. I lost all hope. Then Thomas got me back into the Marines. All I wanted was to lose myself in my work. That's how I didn't believe that it could be better. Then I met you, Ben, and your kids. It was then when I knew. It doesn't matter how bad a situation gets; it never storms forever."

"Lincoln, I'm so sorry. If I had known that before, I would've made you feel more at home. Wherever your daughter is, I'm sure she would've been proud of you no matter what."

"That was eighteen years ago. There's not a day that goes by that I don't curse myself for not holding onto her hand tighter."

Veronica walked around Ben's bed to hug Lincoln. She always knew his daughter mysteriously disappeared, but she never knew how it happened.

"I have always sworn my right hand to Christ himself," Lincoln said, holding Veronica's hand. "If I ever find my daughter again, I'm going to find out who or what took her away from me. Then I'll end them myself." He turned to face Veronica.

"Do you mind if I could talk to Ben alone? I'll only be a few minutes," he asked politely.

"Take as long as you like," she said. She turned and walked out of the room, closing the door behind her. He turned to his best friend.

"Look at you," he began. "What did I say what would happen if you came along, ya dumb-ass?" He tried laughing but stopped. "I know you can't hear me, but on the off-chance that you can, please know that I will avenge what happened you. That Golden Spector guy is gonna have his back broken and you can rest easy.

"But I need you to keep fighting, too," he continued. "If you don't, who are your kids gonna look up to? They can't just have a mom. They need a dad, too. It takes two to make a child whole. I'm old-fashioned like that. I've always looked up to you, Ben. The amount of times you've been blown up, shot at, and shot down and walk away from it all is unbelievable to me. If you can walk away from a grenade explosion, then you can overcome this."

He got up and walked to the door before pausing and turning around to look at him one last time.

"Heroes come in many shapes and sizes, buddy. There's no reason why you shouldn't be one, too." He opened the door and walked through it. Out in the hallway, he saw Veronica leaning against the wall.

"Are you okay?" she asked.

"I'll be fine. I just gotta get ready."

"Get ready for what?"

"To find this bastard and bring him to justice."

"Lincoln, please. Let the military handle this. I'm sure Roland has something up his sleeve they can use."

"Yeah. Me."

"What about Clinton? I'm sure he can help."

"He went off the grid."

Midnight in Iraq. Swarms of people from other countries had banded together, having sworn to kill whomever got in their way.

The village was now a dark, cruel, and unforgiving place full of sin and misery. Five American soldiers were lined up in a circle among the townspeople. Their hands and feet were tied, and a handkerchief had been stuffed in their mouths to prevent them from screaming. In front of the circle was a platform, upon which Hakim grasped Excalibur tightly. The captured Americans could feel the toxic air in their bones. The townspeople were cheering and lifting their weapons in the air. Several of them fired them into the sky. Hakim wanted fear to paralyze the captured Americans as long as possible. The Iraqis were throwing wood near the prisoners' feet.

Hakim smiled and lifted the sword. A giant golden flash of light blasted into the sky and silenced the people at once. Everyone froze and stared. He was their leader and savior. He looked at his audience and stepped down from the platform.

"The Souls of Death are a force to be reckoned with but have never before achieved our true potential," he said. "Thanks to this magnificent weapon, we will be unstoppable. Power like this only comes from Allah. I think we're in His favor now, at last."

The audience erupted in applause.

Hakim slowly approached the bound Americans. He glared into the eyes of each soldier individually. One of the five was female, and Hakim stopped in front of her. He removed the handkerchief from her mouth. "Well, it looks like we have a lady here. What's your name?"

"My name is Sophia Chapel," she said. "I'm the squadron leader of this unit. We've defeated many like you before. You're no different."

"So the pretty flower has thorns? But that nasty attitude is going to get you in trouble. I'm in a good mood today, so I'm gonna ask you a question. Think it through. Your answer might save your whole unit."

She stared at him with disgust.

"Tell me where Lincoln Thaw is," he demanded.

"Mr. Thaw is a well-respected man and one of the best sniper in the Marines," she said. "He'd kill you in a second. You're nothing but a parasite compared to him."

"You try to infiltrate my country and kill my people," Hakim said, chuckling. "And I'm the parasite? You're sadly mistaken."

"He's highly trained and and among the best in his class," Sophia said. "He's the best sniper America has had in a long time. You're no match for him."

"Oh, I know, sweetheart. I know." Hakim slowly stepped back up onto the podium and grabbed hold of Excalibur. At once, he turned and threw the weapon at Sophia's chest. The blade pierced her ribcage, and the tip of the blade exited her back. Blood oozed from her torso. The soldiers in her unit screamed muffled cries.

The crowd erupted again in applause, and Hakim raised his arm toward Excalibur. He sensed its energy from her lifeless corpse.

"Burn them, my children," he yelled. "Let's set yet another example of what we do to foreigners who don't agree to our divine terms." He watched with pleasure as the townspeople threw wood at them and poured gasoline over their faces and bodies. They squirmed and pled for forgiveness. Finally, one of the townspeople lit a match and approached the prisoners. The soldiers screamed in defiance as the match was tossed into the space between them. In a flash, the flames engulfed them all and rose up into the sky.

"This is my gift to you, my children," Hakim said.

A moment later, Raheem appeared in front of them, having teleported from deep space. He stepped up to his father and punched him in the jaw. It took Hakim a second to register what had happened. He saw his son and stood up slowly. Hakim's followers all scattered, trying to get away from the enraged prodigal son.

"You have some courage if you're standing up to your own father," he said to him.

"You're no father. You're a monster."

"You see that?" Hakim yelled, pointing at the burning bodies. Raheem turned to look at the corpses.

"That's the ticket to our freedom, and you're standing in the way of it. I cast you out for a reason." Hakim slashed the blade in his son's direction. Raheem quickly teleported and disappeared from view. Hakim looked around in search of his son.

"I know you're watching me, son. You can't hide forever."

"That's where you're wrong." Raheem's voice echoed from the void. Hakim swiveled his head frantically in search of him.

A moment later, Raheem appeared right in front of him and grabbed him by the neck, ripping Excalibur out of his hand. Raheem held him in the air, choking him. Hakim grabbed his boot knife and swung it in one motion, slicing his son's arm. Raheem cried in pain and dropped him, grabbing his arm and watching as the golden aura healed him. His flesh reformed, and the golden aura grew even brighter now. A scowl appeared on Raheem's face as rage overtook him. He realized he had only one mission: kill his father and take back the throne of rightful leadership. Before Raheem could act, Hakim threw a grenade. Everything went black for a couple of seconds. The device blew up in Raheem's face, causing him to revert to his human form.

The sudden shock made him lose focus, and he went hurling into a nearby truck. The entire top half of the truck was smashed in, and Raheem had a gaping wound on his face. The gash spanned from his eye all the way down to his neck. He winced in pain and saw his father charging at him, wielding Excalibur. Raheem couldn't focus in order to use his power and was forced to fight in mortal form.

"You should have never returned here!" Hakim yelled.

He raised the sword high in the air. Raheem moved out of the way before the blade crushed the car hood, shattering the remaining glass of the car. He tried to rise to his feet but struggled against the might of Excalibur. Hakim kept thrusting down hilt-first on Raheem's back until he swore he heard something break. Hakim stood triumphantly over his son and dropped Excalibur next to him.

"I honestly expected more from a person with a gift such as yours. Pick it up," he said.

Raheem struggled and shook, trying to reach out for the sword. As his hand met the hilt, Hakim slammed his foot down on his hand, breaking it. He yelled in pain as Hakim flipped him over.

"You're a worthless, pathetic excuse for a son. Don't worry. Take comfort in knowing you'll soon meet your maker," he said, raising his boot. As Hakim slammed down his foot, Raheem caught it and held it in place.

"You don't even know the meaning of the word 'son.'"

His body gradually reformed before Hakim's eyes. His hand healed itself, and the gash on his face disappeared, leaving a bright glow that emanated from his eyes. His eyes turned a deep vermillion. In that moment, a portal opened beneath him. Raheem lay on the ground, staring at his stunned father. He leaned up and grabbed his father's arms, flipped him, and threw him into the portal before closing it forever without a trace.

Raheem breathed heavily and rose to his feet. There was nothing around him but fire, sand, and a wrecked car. He closed his eyes and heard shuffling in the distance.

He calmed down when he saw the villagers walking slowly from their hiding spaces in the darkness. He watched them carefully. He was surrounded by the townspeople within minutes. Raheem noticed a flashing light in his peripheral vision.

He turned and saw Excalibur lying in the sand where Hakim had dropped it. He walked over to it and picked it up. Everything became clear to him: he had finally overthrown his father and reclaimed Excalibur. He looked at his audience and smiled for the first time. He started to levitate off the ground so he could see everyone and everything. He could feel the power of Excalibur flowing through his veins.

"Friends, family, children," he said. "We are all victims of the same evil. We cower and shake behind the comfort of closed doors because the Americans think we are terrorists. We are not terrorists. We are believers and followers that one day the world will be united under the same glorious belief system. Killing is only optional when we have to enforce the will of Allah. We will take this world one country at a time. We will overthrow America and replace their flag with our own. My father believed in Souls of Death supremacy. I believe in monitored independence. Men, women, and children will never have to worry themselves about a bomb being dropped on them because we are all a world united under one flag. Our flag. Are you with me?"

The audience erupted with cheers and applause, and Raheem basked in the glory.

He raised the sword to the podium claimed from his father and transformed it entirely; the back of the podium moved upward and shifted. The entire podium started to glow, temporarily blinding everyone except Raheem.

After a moment of shifting and changing, along with the sound of grinding metal, a throne stood engraved with markings of the flag that was placed just on top of the throne. The throne was gold and metallic and had markings of Raheem's past life. One scene even depicted his first encounter with Aura. He used his memories to channel his power and create this throne, a symbol of his limitless dominance and command.

The Souls of Death's flag was red, black, and gold arranged in diagonal stripes. The red printed on the left symbolized the blood sacrificed for success in spreading their domain throughout the world. There was an hourglass printed in the middle, black section of the flag that symbolized that time was their ally. Above and below the hourglass, yellow triangles represented fear striking anyone who opposed them. The black stripe signified that death was just a tool, a steppingstone to greatness. Death was the key to domination. Finally, the last, golden stripe of the flag represented the riches that awaited them in victory.

"The world belongs to us, my friends!" Raheem yelled. "Out there is our salvation. Out there is our world, and out there . . . is our purpose!"

The audience crowded the throne as Raheem floated back down and sat upon it. He basked in the glory of their admiration and congratulated himself. His loyal subjects cheered and screamed his name. He lay back and lounged onto his throne, hanging his arm off the armrest. He smiled, knowing that he had this willing army behind him, following him in his quest for revenge on those who dared to oppose him and the Souls of Death.

"All right, Mr. Thaw. You're next on my list. Then after you, your pathetic country," he said with his veins glowing yellow in anticipation.

CHAPTER 9

"IT IS A CURSE TO stay here and meditate among the millions of realities that coincide with one another. However, my mind drifts along with endless knowledge on every piece of information about every earth in the Quintiliverse. Thousands upon trillions of the same person copied and reborn on multiple Earths every nanosecond, and I simply admire them and watch them grow, learn, and inevitably die. My home planet was extinguished eighty-seven-point-six billion years ago when its core finally deteriorated. My species was wise and gentle. We didn't inflict pain upon anyone nor did we wish to. All we had to do was watch, admire, and observe every species, planet, or race we come upon," said Aura. She paused before continuing.

"My race didn't have families as humans define that unit. We were born out of sheer light, and we were brought into existence as adult beings. The second we were conceived, our brains were flooded with the information of the entire universe. Then we grew our knowledge to more intricate matters, such as how many species live in a universe, multiverse, ultraverse, and quintiliverse. No human mind can comprehend the knowledge I possess.

"The Multi-Precinct is a living force. An entity, if you will.

"I was attracted to the vastness of the universe and realized that if I were to remain here to study and observe this place, it would be for all of eternity due to the trillions of lives present in every Earth, changing and shifting throughout the cosmos. From what I understand, the Precinct has been, and always shall be, a part of every universe.

"There is no greater mystery than the one in which I am taking refuge. I have stayed in this place six-point-five billion years, soaking in energy and information. Nostalgia will often creep into my subconscious. I find myself imagining what it would be like had it not been for my planet's self-destruction.

"I know there are more of my kind out there. Finding them is a difficult task. I can detect a distress beacon that is eons away, but once I teleport to wherever the beacon was sent, I discover nothing but the void of space. I grew disappointed worrying that I may never see my kind again.

"After the first two million years of observing the Precinct's majestic powers, I created a hypothesis: what if there was an alternate parallel universe within the Precinct where my planet never suffered its deadly fate? I felt a surge flowing through my heart. You humans refer to this emotion as excitement and, if possible, hope.

"My planet was forged from the energy of a supernova, and eventually, that energy combined and combusted. It created and mixed the energy in the anti-gravity void. Proteins combined while DNA surged around them. Thus, a perfect planetary structure was born. I took it upon myself to investigate how such a universe even existed. I teleported there and found myself engaged in a world that was my own.

"However, I was surprised to learn that if one stays in such a world where an alternate timeline or scenario has been altered, one may lose memory of their original world. The new memories start to solidify themselves inside one's head. It makes anyone believe this is where they belong, when in reality, it never existed for them in the first place. I was fooled into thinking that my world was flourishing in the distant future, creating lifeforms to seek the galaxy and explore grand and new information to be stored in our endless minds. Diversity can be a cataclysmic subject. Realities are like time itself. If one aspect on a specific Earth is changed, that creates another Earth where the opposite decision happened. You humans refer to this as the Schrödinger's Cat theory. Every nanosecond of each moment that passes throughout these galaxies are decisions made by sentient beings, planets, and lower life forms.

"The ability to control and subdue sub-atomic molecular distortion, time manipulation, interplanetary teleportation, and telekinesis is a task that very few of my people learned. Many tried and failed, but it takes a millennium to discover the secrets of our minds. I can change just about anything; however, I cannot change the basic algorithms of life itself. If I were to use my abilities to their fullest potential, I estimate that fifty-eight galaxies would not survive the resulting cataclysmic event.

"That is why, sadly, my kind are either the wisest beings in any known existence or they are the most catastrophically lethal force of life imaginable. My deepest fear of all rests in the dark crevices of my head: *what if someone from my planet decided to use their abilities for acts of prejudice and injustice?* That question is engraved in my head. My planet had beings who abused their knowledge to expose foreign worlds of treason. These individuals who abused their power were sub-atomically demolished by the higher class in order to protect the reality we collectively experienced. The enforcers would maintain order not only for our world, but for the sake of the entire Multi-Precinct." With that, Aura turned to face her visitor.

"I don't understand why you're telling me this."

"Because I've longed to witness other life forms interact with my kind. I have not had this luxury of speaking to another life form since the light of my planet was vanquished. I want to make sure that my past is remembered through other beings. Not just myself. My kind always wanted to spread knowledge throughout the multiverse, but many organisms in this realm are unable to process such information. It is honestly quite disappointing."

"How come you didn't tell my son about your past earlier?" Hakim asked.

"Because your son is a fool. He would only annoy me with his vain attempts to intimidate me. However, there is something I see in you, something that no one else possesses."

"And what's that?"

"Potential."

★ ★ ★

Lincoln, Thomas, and Adam were in the same virtual reality room from earlier. Lincoln was better prepared this time. Before, he didn't know the features the suit had to offer. He had read some of prototype notes, but these proved limited. Adam scurried all around Lincoln, checking the suit's internal components.

"Move your left arm," Adam ordered. Lincoln moved his arm in a circular motion. He heard robotic mechanisms click and rotate.

"What did you do?" Lincoln asked.

"I added a little juice to make your arm movements pack even more of a punch. Your knuckles have sensors that are connected to the joint in your hand so that your bones will be able to withstand maximum compression." Adam observed the black techno-gears moving fluidly, almost as if they were alive.

"Exactly. What on Earth am I gonna be fighting this time?" Thaw asked.

"Something a little more . . . your style," Adam said. He walked away and sipped his coffee before smiling to himself. Thomas raised an eyebrow.

"Hey, Adam. If you don't mind, I want to say some words before we start."

"I'll be in the control room," Adam said.

"Are you sure you want to be thrown back in this thing again?" Thomas asked.

Lincoln hesitated and looked to the ground. After a moment, he looked back up to his friend.

"If I don't do it again, I'll never know how powerful I can actually be with this thing. Who the hell knows what the future holds if I don't continue training?"

"So when you get yourself killed fighting the Spector, then you'll know?" Thomas asked. "Play hero and run the risk of getting yourself killed in hopes you'll make a difference? You've made a difference your whole life. This suit has nothing to do with your talents. Anyways, I'll be in the control room with Adam. But if you want to stop at any point, don't call Adam. Call me. You understand?"

Lincoln shook his head. "Thomas, when life gives you an opportunity to be more than what you are, and to help more people with your gift, wouldn't you take it?"

"What are you implying?" Thomas asked.

"If this was reversed and you got this suit and you were asked to kill a terrorist threatening America and the president himself, wouldn't you do it?" Lincoln asked.

He realized in that moment that Lincoln had a point. He closed his eyes and walked to the door.

"You always did have a colorful attitude," Lincoln joked.

"*Mr. Thaw, if you're done with your pep talk, I'd like to begin our second trial*," Adam's voice echoed over the speakers of the white tiled room.

"Let's get this over with," Lincoln said. He looked up to the speakers to be sure Adam could hear him. Suddenly, another voice echoed throughout the speakers.

"*Remember, man, think of something that pisses you off and use that to your advantage. For me, it works every time*," Thomas's voice said.

"Duly noted," Lincoln said.

"Welcome. This field test will test your agility, strength, and reaction time," said the female voice in Lincoln's earpiece. *"Please feel free to use any weapons at your disposal. HAS is not responsible for death, injury, brain trauma, puncture wounds, infectious injections, and permanent scars. Remember, this test only lasts for three minutes. The highest you can score is a 100 percent. Good luck, and thank you for using HAS, human advancement at its finest. Your test will now begin."*

Lincoln's surroundings changed abruptly. Each tile on the ceiling began to flip around along with the ground, revealing an image of new surroundings. This one was different from his previous training in that this place seemed eerie at nighttime. Thunder crashed above. Tiny embers littered the ground, crackling and fading. Rain pounded the ground. Lincoln put on his mask. He was ready for anything.

"Hello?" he called out into the endless void of thunder and rain. He was about to take his first step until he was halted by a strange light in the darkness. It appeared to be . . . golden. Suddenly, Lincoln's brain engaged, and he knew exactly what was going to happen next. The light grew closer until a black silhouette appeared in front of him.

"Step to where I can see you," he said, grinding his teeth.

The figure stepped closer. He was outlined by occasional flashes of lightning. His arms radiated gold along with his veins.

"Wipe that smirk off your face," Lincoln said. "You know what's coming to you." He squinted in concentration.

The Golden simulation smiled devilishly and cocked his head to the side. How did a computer system make this all seem so real? He threw a punch and struck the Spector in the jaw, forcing him to stumble and stagger backward. The Spector dabbed the blood with his finger, looked at it, and smiled.

"Enough smiling," Lincoln said. He ran up to him, throwing punches in every direction. The Spector dodged every punch. He eventually teleported out of existence. Lincoln looked at the weapon on his wrist and knew what to do. The Particle Solidifier was his only chance of winning against this enemy. He flipped a switch below the top of the watch, and the weapon started to hum. He felt it get hotter with each second. The only noise that could be heard now was the pouring rain and the thunder above. He finally heard a series of clicks coming from the watch. The clicks grew louder and quicker until they stopped for half a minute.

A moment later, a visible shockwave emanated around him, and the air stood still. The rain hung in suspended animation. He admired the strange sight and held out his hand to touch the rain. To his shock, it was solid. He wrapped his hand around a raindrop and attempted to move it, but to no avail. He looked up to notice the Spector mid-jump between portals, but he too was frozen.

"I got you now," Lincoln said. He fired off the mini-gun from his ankle holster and released a rain of bullets. A smile crept onto Thaw's face as the bullets pierced the Spector's leg. The Spector wailed in pain as he hit the ground. Lincoln activated the Solidifier once more and ran up to him while frozen in time. The Spector's body was half dissipated, just before he was about to disappear.

Thaw grabbed him by the neck and turned off the machine, allowing his opponent's body to re-form. Lincoln's hand molded into his neck to prevent him from getting away. He pulled him into the air in a choke hold. The Spector tried desperately to get away, but it was futile. Even if he wasn't the real thing, it still gave him satisfaction.

Suddenly, the Spector smiled and punched Lincoln square in the jaw. Did he not understand that his fist was melded inside his throat? The Spector then dissipated away in a flash. Lincoln surveyed his surroundings slowly and scanned for the menace.

"Hiding from a battle won't solve anything," Lincoln said. "Come out and face me like a man." A moment later, a flash of gold light appeared right in front of him. Thaw wasn't fazed. Only malice filled his head as he watched his foe step right in front of him. Without warning, the Spector threw a punch and knocked Thaw to the ground. Thaw kept his eyes on the embers below him as he tried to wrap his head around what just happened. He closed his eyes and let the rage overtake him. He shot his eyes back open and leapt into the air like a leopard viciously attacking the Spector.

Blow for blow, the pair dueled until the Spector fell to the ground with blood oozing from his mouth and dripping down his forehead. The simulation seemed as if it were all real. It did feel real. The Spector was choking on his own blood as it gushed from his mouth. Thaw walked over to him, ready to finish the job. He grabbed hold of the Spector's lower chin and grasped the top of his head. With one swift motion, his neck snapped, ending the simulation. Thaw zoned out as his surroundings changed in a matter of seconds back to the plain white room.

With every exhalation, he felt as if he had actually just beat his foe. He was growing increasingly angry that it was not actually the Spector. He clenched his fists and felt his heart race. He had so many emotions running through him that he closed his eyes and attempted to regain his composure. He heard Thomas open the door and sprint into the room.

"Thaw, you . . . really showed your true colors out there, huh?" Thomas asked.

Lincoln turned and stared in shock. Thomas noticed that Thaw was growing distressed. He rushed over to his frightened friend and grabbed his arm as Thaw abruptly fell to the ground with a thud. Thomas shook his arm.

"Thaw, Thaw! Come on, buddy. You got to snap out of it!"

Thaw's ears were ringing. His eyes grew wider; he swore he felt as if he was about to have a panic attack. Suddenly, Adam ran into the room with a needle in his hand. He leaped onto the ground and slipped the needle into Lincoln's neck. Lincoln could feel the ringing fading away. He suddenly inhaled so much air that he started coughing.

"What the hell was that about?!" Thomas yelled.

"My sincerest apologies, Mr. Thaw. I should've injected that into your system before you went into the simulation," Adam said, putting the needle back in his jacket pocket.

"That still . . . doesn't answer the question," Lincoln said, breathing heavily.

"That was a neuro psychological inhibitor," Adam said. "It prevents your brain from thinking that what you see is the real thing."

"How come nothing happened when he fought that big ape?" Thomas asked.

"Because I slipped it into his drink before he went into the system," Adam reluctantly responded. Suddenly, Lincoln shot up and reached for Adam's neck until his body suddenly gave out and he passed out onto the ground.

CHAPTER 10

"MOTHER, I DON'T WANNA LEAVE!" Raheem yelled.

"Honey, I need you to trust Mommy. You need to run as far away from here as you can!" Raheem's mother screamed. Tears streamed down her face from her bloodshot eyes. Raheem was so confused. His father's shouts filled the air. Raheem snapped his head back as he watched his father storm into the room, his face awash with murderous fury.

"Boy, step aside," Hakim said. He picked up Raheem and threw him to the other side of the room like a ragdoll. His skull cracked against the wall. Blood trickled down his cheek, and he lifted his head. Raheem's mother flinched. She couldn't defend herself or her son from her enraged husband's wrath.

"Who the hell do you think you are? You keep my son away from me when you know he must help the cause? He is going to be the leader of the Souls of Death, and you keep him away from me? You sicken me to the bone, Alia. Every time I need to teach him the code of our people, you shelter him from me!"

"I do that because you are a monster."

Hakim backhanded his wife so hard on the left cheek that she toppled over and fell to the ground. She struggled to get up, but Hakim kicked her repeatedly. Raheem tried to help her, but he kept falling down from the pain and blurry vision.

"Raheem, let me show you what happens when someone goes against the Souls of Death," he said, pulling out his pistol. He aimed it at her head and pulled the trigger with a sinister smile on his face.

"No!" Raheem yelled.

He shot upright in bed, sweat dripping down his fear-stricken face, his eyes glowing crimson. His powers were erratic when he slept. He had always been scared to approach his father. He was still haunted now, even after sending his father into the multiverse.

He leaned over and sat on the side of his bunk with the moonlight hitting his back. The golden mist that shrouded his upper body dissipated like smoke. His eyes slowly returned to their normal brown. He put one hand up to his face and tried to regain his composure and breathed slowly to concentrate. He turned around and glared at the moon, staring intently, wondering where Aura was and how she was surveying his situation.

"I need to know for sure," he muttered.

He closed his eyes and began to glow. A moment later, he suddenly vanished. He reappeared in front of Aura, who was exactly where he last saw her, floating in the void of space with her arms stretched out and her eyes closed, concentrating on the life force around her. Aura opened her eyes at once and spoke to him without surprise.

"Hello, Raheem," Aura said calmly.

"Where is my father?" he asked curtly.

"Your father is currently in a place far beyond human knowledge," Aura responded.

"That doesn't even come close to answering my question," Raheem said angrily.

"Your repeated attempts to present anger as a way of getting answers is faulty. I would advise you ask in a more appropriate manner," Aura said, floating nearer to him.

For the first time, Raheem felt intimidated. He had never been this close to her. Aura stopped in front of him. He was now within arm's length of her, staring into her eyes as if she was reading his soul.

"Fine. Where's my father?" Raheem asked more calmly.

"Your father is attempting to increase his moral skills by honing his strengths," she responded.

"He's what?" Raheem asked.

"I sent him to a place where he could spend the rest of his existence learning from his mistakes without hurting others."

"Where'd you take him?" Raheem asked again. His teeth were grinding in controlled rage.

"I sent him to the future. The twenty-fifth century, to be exact. There, he will know the wrongs he has bestowed upon others. I know what you are thinking, Raheem. Why would I act upon another being when it is against the law of my own people? No, we are not permitted to show prejudice against any being of any race. Nevertheless, we are allowed to imprison those who do wrong to other living beings. I have executed this action to 78,556 species throughout my lifetime," Aura stated.

"You're contradicting yourself."

"You're mistaken. Every action my race used to take was for the betterment of the Multiverse, whether it was to transport a deadly black hole from one end of a solar system to the other without endangering any species, or simply moving a meteorite away from a planet rich with life. But what I did to your father had to be executed to ensure he wouldn't do any more harm. I saw potential in him to be a better human being."

"You sadistic—" Raheem started.

"I will conclude this dispute so that you may no longer distract me from my observance of the Precinct. You were raised by a man who was savage in nature and thought the only way to achieve peace was by war. You believe I'm the sick one? Why don't you recall the memories of your father and tell me otherwise? It's such a shame you were raised by that version of your father. You could've been raised by alternative versions where he was a doctor, teacher, firefighter, and much more. The possibilities are limitless. But sadly, it was decided that you would be the son of the worst version possible. There are 3,435,556 versions of your father. All of which were generally acceptable men except one."

"That doesn't make me feel any better. You stated to me before that it was against the law of your own people to interfere in any way. You want to know what you just did. You interfered not only in my father's destiny, but also in mine. And just because you watch over everything in the Ultraverse or whatever, you think you're Allah? You're nothing like Him! You're a pacifist who takes people and ruins their—"

Suddenly, Raheem faded away. Aura turned and looked up into the stars.

"If only you could perceive things as I see them. Then your viewpoint would greatly differ forever," Aura said. She levitated back toward the stars to meditate within her domain of worlds. Raheem teleported back into the moonlight that was shining brightly onto his chest, surrounded by darkness.

" . . . lives, and you just automatically think you're better?" Raheem screamed. A moment later, his demeanor calmed as he realized he was back in his cot. "The next time I see her, it's over," he growled. He lay back onto his bed, thinking about everything that had happened.

He wanted to get back at Lincoln for almost killing his father and stealing what the Souls of Death needed to achieve glory. He knew his father was always an arrogant bastard, but deep down he always knew it was for a purpose. It was to lead them to victory at all costs.

Excalibur was the key. Raheem leaned over and admired the mighty sword on the back wall. He watched as its luminescent golden light emanated with a low hum.

"I have to try," he said to himself, now wide awake. He stared at the blade and closed his eyes to summon his powers. He concentrated more rigorously until he opened his eyes to find the sword was no longer glowing. His powers were practically nonexistent. He tried hard to activate his abilities, but all attempts were futile.

"Aura. She did this. That god-awful scumbag took my powers from me!" Raheem yelled. "Why would she do this to me?" Suddenly, his head erupted with such unbearable pain that he fell to the ground with ringing in his ears. He tried to open his mouth to scream, but to his shock, he couldn't use his voice. He stood up and froze.

"*The reason I have subdued your abilities is rather simple. You don't utilize them properly,*" Aura said.

"*Get out of my head!*" he thought as he tripped over his bed, falling to the ground.

"*I will, only on one condition.*"

"*What . . . in . . . the—? I'll listen. I'll listen! Just stop this god-awful pain,*" he thought.

"*You will deliver Excalibur to its destination of origin and leave it there. It has come to my attention that your race's future is in grave danger if Excalibur remains in use. That sword will eventually lead to this planet's destruction. Seven hundred eighty-nine thousand parallel Earths have just been eliminated within the past one hundred twenty seconds. They all had the same unfortunate endings. The similarity between them all? You never get Excalibur back to its place of origin. Or you refuse me, and I let you destroy your planet under your own free will.*"

"*I promise, okay? I promise I'll get your damn sword back!*" Raheem replied in his head.

"*When the human known as James Clinton was appointed to protect Excalibur, he was given these words: 'You are the Guardian of Excalibur. Watch and protect the blade. Should evil arise and take control, look for the place which holds the scroll.'*"

"*You want me to find a scroll?*" Raheem asked.

"That would be affirmative, Mr. Gorroff. Once you have achieved this, I will grant your powers back to you."

"Fine. Then, um, consider it done." But if the world was in danger, he had no choice. Suddenly, all the pain disappeared, along with the brain-melting migraine.

He stood up and felt the blood rush to his head. What did the world ever give him? It never helped him when his mother was killed. It never helped when his father abused him. It never even helped when he was fighting alongside his brothers in the Souls of Death. All he had to do was pretend to save the Earth until he reached the supposed scroll.

"Just take Excalibur to the place where some scroll is, and after that, it's just a matter of holding this world hostage," Raheem said to himself. A smile crept over his face. Sooner or later, he would rule this world with an iron fist.

★ ★ ★

Lincoln Thaw laid on the hospital bed, unconscious. Monitors surrounded him, beeping in a stable rhythm. Thomas sat on his chair with his arms crossed and a string of drool dripping out of his mouth.

Lincoln's eyes were crusted shut after having spent the last two days in a catatonic state. He struggled to open them. When he did, fluorescent light flooded his pupils. He moaned and tried to get up. His suit was gone, and he was instead wearing elastic purple shorts. He looked around him and realized that he was in a hospital room. The fan rotated above him, sending a nice cool breeze throughout the room. His legs were stiff as he tried to move them. Faint voices came from the other side of the door, letting him know he wasn't totally alone. He laughed at the sight of Thomas, dead asleep in the chair with a magazine in his hand. He leaned over and smacked his knee to wake him up. Thomas bolted upright, dropping the magazine.

"I'm awake!" Thomas yelled. He looked down at Lincoln, who was laughing so hard his already bruised ribs hurt. Thomas got up and walked over to him.

"Morning, Sleeping Beauty. How you feeling?"

"Better. What happened? One minute I was fine, and the next I felt like my head was about to explode." Lincoln squinted and flopped his head back onto the pillow.

"That jackass forgot to inject some sort of serum into your system that keeps you sane in the simulation."

Lincoln shook his head and rubbed his eyes.

"Listen, we have to find the Spector ASAP," Thomas said. "The whole country's on high alert waiting for something to happen."

"Where was he last seen?" Lincoln asked.

"A drone was flying overhead and saw him in Iraq with flags and a throne. This guy's a full-blown tyrant."

"Well, that's what dumbasses do when they have too much power and they want to demonstrate their dominance." Lincoln inhaled and tried to move his stiff legs to the floor. He winced in pain.

"Don't push yourself too hard," Thomas said, grabbing his arm and helping him up.

"Bub, you seem to forget that I've sat in molten hot sand in the middle of the desert for days on end before getting shot at. Believe me, if I can do that, then I can walk away from this." Thaw rose and stood on his bare feet. "We need to get to Roland Industries pronto."

"What the hell are they gonna do?" Thomas asked.

"They're the world's leading tech company of our time. There's no problem they can't fix."

"Then how come we haven't won this war?"

"Because too many lives are at risk. We need to tell Roland's CEO."

"You mean Charlie Roland? The richest man in the world? The same man who bought out Google?"

"Yes, Thomas. I'm going to see him personally."

"Hate to break it to you, man, but he's a busy guy. He's the executive of, what, only fourteen different corporations? Including every gunmetal material the military uses?"

"Thomas, it's me. I have connections. I'll find a way. I always do."

"I'm telling you, man. It's gonna be difficult."

"That's what makes our job so satisfying, right? Finding a way around the problem. Now help me find my shoes."

Charlie Roland stood before the gargantuan glass window that overlooked the lights of the city. Raindrops poured down on the glass, and the gray-blue sky appeared to be in mourning. Charlie watched the city intently, standing motionless with his hands folded behind his back. Whenever he found himself with a lot on his mind, he would go to the window and look over the city. He had been thinking about Clinton for the past few days. The only sound in his office was from the storm.

The dark clouds reflected off his patent leather shoes. His pants were impeccably pressed, and his blazer was crisp, perfectly tailored. He closed his eyes and listened to the sound of rain. It soothed him.

"Mr. Roland, there is a video transmission on line one," said an electronic voice, interrupting his trance.

Roland exhaled, annoyed. He made it clear to his staff that he wanted no interruptions while he was relaxing. Obviously, someone couldn't listen to his directions. Suddenly, a bolt of lightning lit up the sky before him.

"Lights on. Windows closed. View transmission," Roland said.

The room shifted. His office was trimmed with polished wood. Two glass windows were at the left side of the room, and two of the other panes faced the city to the right. The walls were covered with antique oil paintings of both his esteemed family members, and his family's land from the early 1800s. Behind him rested a tiny wall cabinet stocked full with champagne, shot glasses, wine bottles, and goblets. No one ever touched his cabinet.

He was a tall, elegant man in his late fifties with slicked-back hair. He sat down in his chair and tapped the surface of his PAD Z. When the company bought out Apple, they wanted to oversee every upcoming product they would distribute to the world. They took the blueprints of the iPad Pro and combined the Apple computer chip together to make an even better, more efficient version. The PAD Z was capable of receiving and making holographic calls to anybody, anywhere in the world.

The PAD Z projected an image from his desk into the open space on the rug. A holographic Lincoln Thaw stood in the middle of the room with his hands in his pockets.

"How are you, sir?" Lincoln asked, his voice fading in and out. Thaw was nervous talking to the man who owned half of the world's military supplies and weaponry.

"Hello, Mr. Thaw. Lincoln Thaw, is it?" Roland asked. "I've heard a lot about you. Sixty-seven confirmed kills, forty-three successful missions in Arabia and Pakistan. You've been quite busy."

"Well, all I do is protect the innocent and serve the best nation on the face of the planet, sir. Nothing more."

"What do I owe this glorious pleasure of speaking with such a fine soldier from Uncle Sam?"

"Sir, are you aware of the Golden Spector?"

"Yes, I am," Roland groaned. "I'm spending millions of dollars in military soldiers and weapons to kill him before he does something that'll bring the country to its knees."

"Well, sir, I'm looking to find him myself and neutralize him before he does any more damage. I know I'm only one in millions that wants him dead, but I firmly believe I can achieve that."

"Thaw, I'm not sure you realize how powerful this individual is. This man has the ability to traverse vast distances without a second's hesitation. Take no offense, sir, but you're only human. What makes you so special without a sniper rifle at your side?"

"I almost murdered his father. He hates me, and I know that. So why not use his arrogance and rage to our advantage?"

"Well, I guess you two have had some history together, huh? Here's what I'll do. You are aware of the weapon called the Particle Solidifier, yes?" Roland rose from his chair.

"Yes, sir, I've had the honor of testing it myself."

"My weapons development crew had labored extensively in creating that particular device. But recently I asked for a slight modification."

"Well, actually, sir, I've had the privilege of testing this prototype, and I have developed a level of proficiency with its mechanics."

"Can I count on you to bring him to justice?"

"Yes, sir, I can't afford to fail."

"Okay, great. Losing someone is never easy. Especially if they mean the world to you."

"How'd you know about that, sir?" Thaw asked.

"I read a case file on you before you called. I gotta say, you've been through a lot. I hope you don't mind. I like to know a person before I talk to them virtually."

"Sir, what are you implying? I don't think I understand."

"All I'm saying is that you're a unique soldier with nothing to lose. Don't let something little get in the way of your greatness. I'll see you around, Thaw. End transmission," Roland said.

"Mr. Thaw, you will be a fine specimen for study," he said. He picked up a goblet and filled it with wine, smiling to himself as he sipped and turned to face the dark sky.

CHAPTER 11

"WHERE ARE THOSE DAMN PLANS?" Raheem cursed aloud. He rifled through his father's old desk full of doomsday weaponry blueprints. Maps were scattered throughout his father's quarters. Mythology papers littered the floor with government documents accompanying them. These files contained detailed records of Excalibur and possible whereabouts of other mythological artifacts. Raheem's father had been obsessed with finding these relics.

The desk he was scouring was ravaged by time. Raheem slammed his hands on the desk in frustration, scattering a pile of documents. He closed his eyes to collect himself. When he reopened them, he looked over and noticed one file that had been at the bottom of the stack. Curiously, he placed the books and files on the desk and picked up this strange, sunbaked file.

Classified: Top Secret: The Circulation of This Document Shall Be Limited to Select People Who Perform Their Duties

"What in the—" He opened it slowly and read the bold text. A minute later, he had become lost in the secret files before him.

CIA
Central Intelligence Agency

Country: ▮▮▮▮▮

Date: 4 Dec 1923
Publish Date: ▮▮▮▮▮▮▮▮
Language: Greek
Official Information: Yes
Disclosed Information: No
No. Of Pages: 1

▮▮▮▮▮▮▮▮▮▮▮ Found in ▮▮▮▮

Document Case File: 224E8

According to Doctor Gerald Spencer, this document is aimed to specially address the discovery of the ▮▮▮▮ found in Southern Greece. Spencer departed from America on Nov. 12, 1923, to Greece to study a new form of bacteria. He traveled into the woods until he stumbled over something mysterious. He noticed that the strange ▮▮▮▮ had ▮▮▮▮▮▮ and ▮▮▮▮▮ branded on the perimeter. He took numerous pictures of the ▮▮▮▮ and had them in his possession until he contacted the authorities and the images were revoked from his possession ever since. The ▮▮▮▮ has been placed under government watch for ▮ years and has remained at the ▮▮▮▮▮▮▮▮▮ ▮▮▮▮▮▮ Center, underground away from sight. The ▮▮▮ has had repeated occurrences such as molecular ▮▮▮▮▮▮, blinding ▮▮▮▮▮▮▮▮, and reflections that represent a ▮▮▮▮ with ▮▮▮▮ for hair. ▮▮▮▮▮▮▮▮▮▮

████████████████████████████████████

████ Further investigation is required to better understand the encrypted phenomena. █ scientists from around the globe took part of attempting to mandate it. Year of origin is unknown at this time of writing this. David Witherspoon (scientists from ████ ██████████) was the first human being to interact with the ████ and live. He kept saying that he saw visions of a man with a sword and shield towering over a man emanating gold. Witherspoon suffered severe seizures and eventually died on ██████ 1941, to a heart attack caused by the numerous seizures. Many attempted to study Witherspoon's brain patterns and replicate the process to see what the █████ showed him, but every attempt was faulty, leading to death. No further information has been disclosed onto this document as of now.

"How can this be possible? There's another relic?" Raheem felt as if he was going to throw up. He clenched his other fist and slammed the table. He screamed in rage and noticed other case files slipping out of the folder. He angrily grabbed one and read it over.

FBI

Federal Bureau of Investigation
Document Case File: 225H6
- Country: Guadalupe Island
- Date: █ Oct 1910
- Publish Date: ██████████████
- Language: ████████
- Official Information: Yes
- Disclosed Information: No
- No. Of Pages: 1

Mysterious ▮▮▮▮▮▮▮▮ Overtakes ▮▮▮▮

Regarding the recordings of Dr. Richard Davis, he traveled to Guadalupe Island to study a strange phenomenon ▮▮▮▮▮ ▮▮ ▮▮▮▮▮▮▮▮▮▮▮▮▮▮▮▮▮▮▮▮▮▮▮▮ Once there, he scavenged the area looking for the source of the strange pulse. He used a metal detector amplified to detect large quantities of sound in the area and found a lead. ▮▮▮▮▮▮▮▮▮▮▮▮▮▮▮▮▮▮▮▮▮▮▮▮▮▮▮ ▮▮▮▮▮▮▮▮▮▮▮▮▮▮▮▮▮▮▮▮▮▮▮▮▮▮▮▮▮▮▮▮▮ He found a ▮▮▮▮▮ buried under ▮▮▮▮▮▮▮▮▮▮ and discovered where the anomalies came from. He was able to dig the ▮▮▮▮ up and contacted the military. They transported him and the ▮▮▮▮ back to America for further investigation. The ▮▮▮▮ was placed under constant surveillance and was tested for radiation. The ▮▮▮▮▮ was found glowing and caused one of the assistants to see ▮▮▮▮▮▮▮▮▮▮▮▮▮▮▮▮▮▮▮▮▮▮▮▮▮▮▮▮▮▮▮▮ The assistant later died from the extreme seizure, and the ▮▮▮▮ was put under ice to minimize the beacons for good. Until this day, the ▮▮▮▮ has ceased any and all disruptions. At the time this document was written, the ▮▮▮▮ is still being kept under cryogenic stasis until further notice.

Raheem felt his rage transform into curiosity as he re-read the entire document in disbelief. How could there have been multiple relics that slipped under the radar? How could he have been so careless to ensure that all the relics were recovered and seized? Raheem tried to understand the significance of all these locations and doctors. He went back and re-read the last document, still in shock. He suddenly spotted two more folders stacked on each other on the corner of the desk as he hovered over it. He pushed the folders away to read for another time. He couldn't take any more surprises. His curiosity turned into rage once more, and he thrusted his arm across the desk, sending everything on it tumbling across the room. He screamed in frustration and scanned the remaining papers on the floor. He knew that the more time he wasted, the better chance Thaw had of finding him first. He had to act now before it was too late.

He stormed out of his father's tent and lost himself in the stars. He had to collect himself before doing anything else. He had suffered from bipolar episodes since he was little. Seeing his mother's murder had pushed him over the edge.

"Aura, I know you're watching me right now. I know you despise me. I know you're all powerful, and I am nothing compared to you. But there's one thing that separates us. Deep down, you care about life of any kind. But I do not. You can do everything in your power to stop me, erase me, or shun me out of existence. But there will always be another version of me that will rise from below. Thousands of versions of me will show you that humans can be a powerful force. You . . . you are no god. You're just a pathetic excuse for a guardian."

Somewhere far away, Aura drifted through the metaphysical cosmos, concentrating on everything her brain was hardwired to consider. Suddenly, she tuned into what Raheem had said to her. Aura smiled. She knew what further plans he maintained and was aware they weren't too friendly. Aura could see he was a hazard to life itself.

Meanwhile back on Earth, Raheem smiled at the sky, knowing that Aura heard him. In that moment, he felt stronger than ever. He watched the stars like they were distant enemies to be vanquished. Raheem slowly walked back into his tent and lay down on his cot. The tent was very small, with the ceiling and wall crumbling as if caving in on itself. He glared over at the golden sword, which leaned against the wall as if waiting for him to pick it up. Raheem smiled and knew what he was going to do next. He reached down into a lower shelf below the desk and brought out a map of Iraq. He placed his finger on a single blue line, which he traced until he hit a red dot. He knew this signified good news. There was an airstrip nearby. If he worked diligently, he knew it was his for the taking. All he had to do was follow the path the sword told him to take. He could commandeer one of the combat trucks and overtake one of the jets. It was a foolproof plan.

"Ben," Raheem mumbled. He had almost forgotten the name of the man he almost killed. He closed his eyes and relished the thought of his enemy mourning his comrade.

He walked over to the sword and grabbed the hilt, lifting it and sliding it into his scabbard. He sprinted out the door, crushing the sand under his toes. He spotted one of the trucks in the distance and raced to it, clambering through the door and sitting down. He removed Excalibur from the scabbard and tossed it onto the passenger seat.

He reached down and grabbed the key beneath his driver's seat. Every loyal member of the Souls of Death knew to leave the keys to any vehicle beneath the seat in case they were under attack. He put the key in the ignition and twisted it. The truck rumbled to life, the headlights turning on, brightening the night. He pulled the shifter downward into drive and slammed the gas. The truck lumbered into the empty darkness, where he would resume his descent into evil.

He drove for miles, anticipating every turn after memorizing the map. He'd be there in no time. After half an hour, he finally reached the front security gates. He floored the accelerator at the sight of them, smashing through them and driving until he found the jet he was looking for, an F-15E Strike Eagle. It stood tall, overlooking the base with silent pride. Raheem squealed the truck to a stop and grabbed the sword before sprinting to the jet. He climbed the ladder and opened the cockpit, sitting inside and placing the sword carefully down by his legs. He flipped a few switches, and the cockpit came to life around him; a few more controls started the engines, and one final switch lowered the glass cockpit until he heard it *click* in place. A moment later, he had veered the F-15E Strike Eagle right and was taxiing down the runway.

By the time he had the bird in the air, he knew he would be successful. He flew higher and higher until he was above the clouds. He leaned over and activated a weapon that was rarely used and was developed by Roland Industries. The entire jet quickly covered itself with tiles that camouflaged itself in the moonlit night. Benjamin Frost had no idea of the doom that would shortly unfold before his eyes.

CHAPTER 12

"THE SUIT'S READY," ADAM SAID, marveling at it with pride. Thomas and Lincoln stood next to him, crossing their arms. The suit was under a giant glass dome. Adam worked around the clock to improve the suit's exterior, making it more agile and refining its integrated, fully functioning arsenal.

"It looks so much better. What did you do, Adam?" Lincoln asked.

"Oh, a little here and there," Adam said sarcastically. Lincoln and Thomas shot him a look. "Well, the mask has been refitted to memory metal. It can withstand heavy artillery and explosions. Your face will quite literally feel nothing," he said.

"Well, put me on the officially impressed list," Lincoln said, nodding in amazement. "Don't stop there. What else have you done?"

"Well, the arms also have two implanted coats of memory metal that can withstand twice the amount of pressure that the human body can normally withstand for when you go to fight the Spector. He can teleport, but there's one thing that you have that he doesn't.

Hidden explosives. There's a small hidden button on the joint of each index finger that, once pressed, detonates from the exoskeleton of the suit. It causes a chain reaction that destroys anything within a five-foot radius."

Lincoln and Thomas froze in shock. They stepped closer to the glass to gawk at the subtle gadget.

"There's more to it than that," Adam continued. "The chest has reinforced titanium that is blended with synthesized Chobham armor."

"You mean the stuff they make tanks out of?" Thomas asked.

"Yes, thanks to Roland Tech, I was able to synthesize the metals and increase the strength by 12 percent. So it should be able to stop a speeding bullet."

"How was Roland Industries even able to do that?" Thomas asked, staring. "Normally, we're the first people to be notified about this kind of stuff."

"They wanted to keep this new alloy under wraps. The government didn't want anyone else using it. It was too strong, and I was one of the only people that had clearance to work with it."

"What else does it have?" Lincoln asked.

"The belt has all sorts of gadgets that I think you'll love. To the left, you have flash grenades. The canisters have rings that cause temporary blindness. You can do a lot of damage by the time it wears off. Once you pull the canister from your belt, a mechanism sends a signal to the mask, and your eyes will be shielded from the effects. To your right is a lovely device of my own invention. It's called a Mini-Electrode."

Lincoln leaned in and admired the small, circular device that was attached to the other thigh. It was silver around the perimeter and blue in the center. It had such a simple design compared to everything else in the suit.

"And what exactly is a Mini-Electrode?" Lincoln asked.

"When you press the blue button, it initiates an electrical current that travels through your suit and to your gauntlet. It sparks an electrical charge every time you deliver a punch. So basically every time you throw a punch, the other guy loses some brain cells."

"Dirty boxing?" Thomas asked. "You know that comes in handy."

"How much damage exactly do these . . . electrodes do?" Lincoln asked, crossing his arms.

"Each punch can break a cinder block," Adam said. "It puts brass knuckles to shame."

Lincoln took a second to process this. If he had that much power, he could take on anything. He had to be careful whenever he used that in the future. One false move could be fatal.

"Anything else on the legs?" Lincoln asked, surveying the rest of the suit. Thomas pondered the same question.

"There are braces that cover your knees to protect you from damaging impacts," Adam stated. "These joint shields allow you to jump to heights of as much as fifty feet. Also, this suit allows you to run at speeds up to fifty miles per hour. These braces will help you easily catch enemies in both stealth and combat missions."

"How the hell did you get this tech from Roland?" Thomas asked. "I thought they made it illegal for any soldier to have something like this."

"Roland has made an exception due to the dire situation with the Spector," Adam said.

"Where's the Particle Solidifier?" Lincoln asked.

Adam was caught off guard. He walked over to the wall and waved his hand over it. A holographic keypad appeared, and he started to tap in a few numbers. The two other men raised their eyebrows as the wall hissed and moved. A tiny compartment opened, and out slid a little piece of metal with a brown Velcro strap. It was the size of a wristwatch, with four dials on it with all different symbols and number readings. He picked it up from the mini-platform and walked over to Thaw.

"Give me your wrist, please," Adam requested.

Lincoln held out his wrist as Adam strapped the device onto

him. With one final click of the strap, the device was activated, and Lincoln felt mild heat radiating from it.

"Every time you activate this, you need to give it some time to idle and warm up. If you don't, the events could be catastrophic."

"What do you mean, catastrophic?" Thomas asked.

"Imagine life as we know it stuck in one moment forever without ever moving," Adam answered.

"How frequently can I use this?" Lincoln asked.

"I tried my hardest to reconfigure the electronics to make it work more frequently, but the maximum amount of time you have is thirty seconds for each burst of particle deceleration."

"Thirty seconds?" Lincoln asked. "What am I supposed to do in just thirty seconds?"

"That's why I gave you all these other gadgets to fight," Adam said.

Lincoln examined the device strapped to his wrist.

"The four gauges on the solidifier are for four different measurements," Adam started.

"There better be a manual for all this, I swear," Lincoln said.

Thomas stood dumbfounded. It was so much information at once.

"Oh, there will be. I'm going to make one for you, but for now all I have are my personal notes."

Lincoln shook his head, waiting for Adam to continue.

"The top left dial tells you how much time you have until you can use it effectively again. If the right dial reads *F*, the device has enough power to sustain you. However, if it reads *E*, you better let it charge ten minutes or it could explode. The bottom left dial tells you how much time you have until the environment around you returns to normal. Finally, the last dial tells you about how many people there are within a ten-foot radius of you."

Not only was Lincoln overwhelmed, but he couldn't get over the fact that he was graduated from being an average sniper to an advanced mechanized super-soldier, accompanied with the newest technology. He took a deep breath and tried to remember everything. His train of thought was suddenly interrupted by an ear-piercing noise from the ceiling above.

★ ★ ★

"What's that?" Thomas asked.

"The Emergency Alert Program," Adam said. He spun on his heels and sprinted from the room. Thomas and Lincoln ran after him into the small, metallic hallway as red emergency lights flashed around them. The two men halted in their tracks as they entered the room where Adam had stopped. Computers of all kinds were everywhere. The screens ran through all kinds of data, and some showed a global view of the world's energy readout. Adam stood hunched over a screen, looking distraught

"Adam, what's going on?" Thomas asked.

With one swipe of a hand, Adam transferred what he was seeing onto the jumbo screen that faced the room. NBC News suddenly flashed onto every screen in the room. Lincoln and Thomas froze in fear and rage.

"This is Jessica Dotson reporting live. Half of Norfolk, Virginia, has been decimated by a jet from the terrorist group known as the Souls of Death. The aircraft has sent three missiles through retirement homes, killing an estimated one hundred and forty-five people, and the death toll is still rising. Debris litters the streets, and the military has initiated action—"

Suddenly, a loud crash accompanied by screams could be heard in the distance until static swarmed the screens. Adam slowly lifted his head to face the TV. The room was dead silent except for the crackling of static. An image suddenly returned to the screen. It was the bloody face of a deceased woman, her beautiful forehead now oozing with blood. Her eyes were closed, and her mouth gaped open. In the background lay the ruins of a war zone. Dust clouded the area, and the roar of a jet echoed through the horrific scene.

Adam leaned over and tapped another button, turning off the

channel entirely. He leaned away from the table and paced over to the two men.

"We failed," he said. "More people were killed. We can't do anything more. Instead of actually getting out there and stopping the problem, I wasted my time making a suit that only one person can wear and use. Who am I kidding at this point? The Spector has already won."

Lincoln put his hand on his shoulder and looked directly in his eyes.

"One person can make the biggest difference. I'm going to show you that we haven't been doing all this training for nothing." He marched back to the other room and walked over to the suit that still stood safely behind glass.

"All right, it's judgment day," Lincoln said, opening the glass door.

★ ★ ★

Norfolk was being turned into a city of dust and death. Bodies lay in the streets, and buildings were on fire everywhere. The nurses were working diligently to evacuate the patients as the rogue jet caused havoc in the skies above. Only a select few patients remained in the hospital, and the building was relying on generators. The entire Frost family was in the hospital, trying to get past security to reach the third floor. Veronica tried to comfort her children amid the mayhem and destruction, but it was clear they were frightened.

Screams filled the halls as patients were evacuated from their rooms on stretchers. The once brightly lit halls were dim as more stress was placed on the emergency generators. Ben's eyes fluttered open slightly as he heard the distant commotion around him. Everything was blurry and moving fast.

"Hurry, we don't know how much longer this building has until it collapses!" someone shouted down the hall. "Get Mr. Frost out of here now!"

A moment later, he was hastily moved to a stretcher for transport. His vision gradually grew clear enough to read the EXIT sign at the end of the hallway. Suddenly, his confusion turned to a wave of fear. Smoke was spiraling into the heavens. He saw a woman with two small children running up to them. Benjamin sat upright to embrace his family.

"*Daddy*!" his children screamed in unison. Veronica began to sob as she wrapped her arms around all of them. When the kids let go of him, Veronica kissed him deeply. He closed his eyes and felt thankful to be alive.

"What happened?" he asked.

"It's a long story, but we gotta move!" she said. At once, she glanced over at a hulking black shape emerging from the clouds.

"Ma'am, we need to take this man to the nearest hospital immediately," said the nurse pushing his stretcher. "This one's about to collapse." He was covered in ash and blood.

"Nurse, I understand entirely, but he's my husband," Veronica said. "If we stay here any longer, we may all die. I'll take him myself."

The nurse closed his eyes and nodded.

"Go now if you want to take him. Just go!"

Veronica pushed the stretcher, and a moment later, the Frost family was rushing toward their car. Zachary and Theia sprinted alongside their mother.

Just as they reached the car, a sudden explosion knocked them off their feet, hurling them in all different directions. Veronica lay on the concrete a moment later.

What used to be their car was now a smoldering wreck of twisted metal and ash. A missile from the jet above had annihilated their car. Veronica rose and blinked from the impact. She attempted to shake her daughter awake, but Theia was unconscious. She looked to her side and found her husband and son lying face down to the pavement.

To her horror, the jet was landing on one of the carriers in the distance. The air was filled with screaming turbine engines. Minutes passed before the engines cut off entirely. The glass cockpit hissed and slowly raised, and the pilot emerged. The Golden Spector stood inside the open cockpit, smiling devilishly. He reached down, grabbed the sword, and hopped down from the cockpit.

"Only through pain and suffering does your enemy finally give up the will to fight," the Spector said, admiring the smoldering ash of the destroyed city. He carried the golden sword at his side. Veronica knelt next to her motionless daughter.

"Ah, I see now. You're the happily wedded wife of the man I defeated," he said calmly.

Veronica grew angrier by the second. She knew that if she didn't stand up and show she wasn't afraid, she'd at least die protecting her family.

The Spector stepped closer to her, wearing a smug smile. He finally stopped right in front of her. Within an arm's length stood the man responsible for the deaths of millions of people. They stood face to face, staring into each other's eyes. With one swift motion, she slapped him in the face.

"How dare you do this to my family? You're not even worthy of being called a human being!" she cried.

He smiled and snatched her neck with one arm, lifting her with little effort.

"Darling, when you've seen the things I have, and you've been granted gifts beyond all knowledge, your respect for life around you decreases," he said.

He pulled her closer to his face. "At the end of this day, everyone you care for will die." He turned and tossed her into the street. He bent down to pick up Theia.

A moment later, he felt a surge of pain radiating through his back. He was sent flying into a nearby truck. He heard a low, mechanical voice call out to him.

"Stay away from them," the voice commanded. The Spector struggled to stand upright. Within seconds, he was facing his opponent.

There stood a tall, muscular man wearing a black uniform. His fist was clenched, and it sparked with electricity. That was the first time he would use the Electrodes that Adam installed.

"I can't say I'm not impressed," said the Spector. "Who are you?"

"You can call me . . . the Marksman."

Lincoln's anger grew. However, he was trained better than to let trash talk get the better of him. Adam failed to inform him that his voice changed whenever the mask was on. It would reduce the chance of someone recognizing him. The surge of electricity made Lincoln feel invincible. He could tell Raheem was slightly intimidated by his appearance. Lincoln's peripheral vision was full of electronic Readouts:

- *Particle Solidifier Chamber Core: Optimal*
- *Mini Electrode Energy Levels: Optimal*
- *Memory Metal Conditions: Optimal*
- *Systems Check: OK*
- *Facial Analysis: Intimidated*
- *Wanted For: Crimes against Humanity*
- *Facial Recognition Confirmed: Raheem Gorroff*

Lincoln concentrated on Raheem, who clung to the blade. Suddenly, an electronic voice echoed through Lincoln's ears.

"Calculating all possible strategic advancements," the voice stated. The same voice from the simulation. He listened closely to her.

"Calculation successful. You have one hundred thirty-four tactical combinations at your disposal, Mr. Thaw."

Lincoln relished the number of possibilities by which he could win this scenario. The left corner of his peripheral monitors showed his heart rate and brain activity. If something were to happen to him, the line patterns would alert him that something was wrong.

On the right was a rotating holographic image of the electrodes he was using. Whatever weapon he would use, the display of the device would pop up on screen and read out the stats and power levels the weapon.

"Seems like I have a worthy opponent," the Spector said.

The Spector jumped into the air and threw the sword at him

with full force. Lincoln kept his eyes on the blade as he jumped in the air with instantaneous reflexes. He reached out for the blade and waited for the handle to come within reach. He gracefully grabbed the handle and somersaulted to the ground with the tip of the blade piercing the ground. Lincoln knelt there and raised his head to look at his bewildered opponent, who stood speechless.

"You underestimated me, Gorroff," Lincoln said, rising to his feet and holding the sword at his side. "You struck first blood, and you hurt innocent people."

"I must say, I didn't expect you to be so agile," the Spector said. "But nevertheless, I'll dispose of you like I disposed of half the people in Norfolk."

Thaw grew more irate. Nothing bothered him more than a psychopath taking sick pleasure in destroying innocent lives. He raised the sword and chucked it almost as fast as it was thrown to him. Raheem smiled and raised a hand as if something were being handed to him. The blade suddenly froze in midair and was suspended in time. With a flick of Raheem's wrist, the blade split into a million pieces and scattered into the air. The particles twisted through the air and reformed in his hand.

Meanwhile, in the Multi-Precinct, Aura felt a disturbance ripple through existence. She inhibited the abilities of Excalibur and was about to re-summon Raheem, but she stopped when she heard a voice infiltrate her vast and mysterious mind.

"I beat the system," came the sound of Raheem's voice. *"You are not a god."*

Raheem held the sword and smiled. He looked back at the Marksman and aimed the sword at him. A blast emanated from the tip of the blade and threw him off his feet. Thaw landed with his back on a fire hydrant, and a surge of pain radiated up his spine. Raheem watched in delight as his enemy struggled on the ground, and he raised the blade once more.

"You're even more pathetic than you look," he said.

He slashed the blade down, slamming it onto the Marksman's memory metal, which prevented him from being hurt. To Raheem's shock, his opponent grabbed hold of the blade and smacked it out of his hands.

"You're one to talk," he quipped.

The Marksman grabbed hold of Raheem's head, thrusted down, and kneed him in the mouth. He threw Raheem back into the air and punched him so hard that the wind was knocked out him. Raheem got up and raised his hand to summon Excalibur. Thinking fast, Thaw intercepted the handle as it was pulled toward his opponent. With one lurch, the sword propelled itself through the air with Thaw still holding onto it. Raheem clenched his fist and greeted his opponent by punching him square in the face. The punch was so forceful that the interface inside was disabled. Thaw flipped the mask up in order to see properly.

The Spector's face immediately twisted with rage and recognition. The American leader from all those years ago, Lincoln Thaw. Countless emotions sped through his mind: his friend's death, his capture, his own torture in American custody . . .

" . . . you," Raheem seethed.

The sword flew into Raheem's hands, and Thaw leaped into action. He activated the electrodes once more and heard a slow-rising pitch from the device as the power charged. Once the sound stopped, Thaw cocked a fist and tried to punch the terrorist. But he was blocked by Excalibur. A shockwave was sent though the air, shattering all windows in close proximity. The pavement beneath them buckled.

"You're an excellent fighter, but you have much to learn," Raheem said while he swung the blade near his head.

The pair shot into the air. Raheem screamed and punched his face. They landed in a small river away from the battered city and splashed into the water. They continued to fight even as they sunk to the bottom.

Raheem reached out and wrapped his hands around his opponent's throat. Thaw looked up and saw that the surface was becoming less visible. Dots overtook his vision. Suddenly, he reactivated the electrodes, and the Spector convulsed, letting go of his throat. Thaw swam desperately to the surface and left Raheem to drown. As soon as he reached the surface, he gasped for air.

Thaw looked up to the sky and inhaled deeply. The sun was starting to break through the black clouds. The light streamed down to help the battered souls of Norfolk. Raheem lay at the bottom of the lake in darkness. Even the seaweed surrounding him seemed lifeless. Raheem's motionless body rocked back and forth with the flow of the water above. Excalibur lay in the street. A woman walked toward it.

It was Veronica. Her family was rushed to the nearest hospital. Benjamin's body was thrown, blown up, and shot. He didn't deserve this. Her heartbreak was disrupted by the sight of Excalibur on the cracked pavement. She stood, puzzled, then leaned down and picked it up with one hand to admire its beauty. At that moment, a grin slithered across Raheem's face at the bottom of the lake. The sword trembled and glowed. Veronica panicked and dropped the sword as it continued to spasm on the ground.

"What the hell?" she muttered to herself.

Golden flashes began to emanate from Raheem's body. The water around him started to swirl with unnatural currents. Raheem's eyes shot open, and he arched his back. He stood underwater, looking up to the murky surface, smiled wider, and raised his hand to summon Excalibur.

Veronica watched as the blade shot up into the sky and disappeared into the clouds. Thaw swam faster to land. He looked up, and his heart sank. He watched as the sword torpedoed through the sky and splashed into the water. Thaw held his breath and ducked underwater. The sword was nowhere to be found. Blackness surrounded him.

Suddenly, without warning, he felt a surge of power underneath him.

The water around him turned red. He turned and looked at the source of the pain, and his heart dropped. His right leg was oozing blood. The blade cut right through the memory metal.

How could that happen? He thought his armor could withstand anything.

He painfully leaned over and applied pressure to the wound. The deep gash in his leg was visible through the tear in the memory metal. Without warning, the air around him swirled like a hurricane. The water in the river—still fresh with his blood—started to open in a whirlpool. Raheem emerged from the whirlpool with the sword. It glistened in the sun along with Raheem's body. He looked up to the sun and smiled. He then turned and looked down at the bleeding man before him.

"It hurts, doesn't it?" Raheem said. "To be so badly injured. You think because you have toys and gizmos you're somehow stronger than me?" He levitated closer. Lincoln watched in horror as his opponent drew closer.

"Once I kill you, I'm gonna go find the scroll and get all my untamed, raw power back," Raheem said. He raised Excalibur into the air as his temporary foe would be finally vanquished. Thaw closed his eyes under the mask and waited for the inevitable.

He heard the whistle of the blade swing until a gunshot echoed through the air. A moment later, he heard a splash from the river. Thaw opened his eyes to see that Raheem had fallen back into the shallows, a bullet wound in his forehead. Excalibur lay in the water next to him. He whipped his head around to see who'd fired the shot. A familiar woman stood with her hands gripping the handle of a gun. Her clothes were dirty and tattered. It was Veronica.

"Oh my God, are you okay?" she yelled as she tucked the pistol under her belt. Thaw took this opportunity to swim toward land. When he arrived, she fell next to the mystery hero, trying to help him up.

"Thank you for saving my family, but who the hell are you?" she asked. Her eyes went wide as she saw the open wound on his leg. She tried to apply even more pressure to staunch the bleeding. Lincoln was impressed by her calm attitude under pressure. His virtual monitors flashed everywhere in his peripheral vision.

- *Particle Solidifier Chamber Core: Optimal*
- *Mini Electrode Energy Levels: Critical*
- *Memory Metal Conditions: Critical*
- *Systems Check: Critical*
- *Facial Analysis: Concerned*
- *Facial Recognition Confirmed: Veronica Frost*
- *Warning: Emergency Distress Beacon Now Online*

Veronica applied pressure to the wound as she turned to face the masked man. "I'm gonna ask one more time because I have to know, who are you?"

Under normal circumstances, Lincoln wouldn't have revealed his identity. However, this was Veronica Frost. He knew she had every right to know the truth.

"I'll show you," he said. He raised his arms near the back of his neck. He grabbed the edge of the mask and pulled upward. He felt the sun beating down through the dark clouds. Silence filled the air. He slowly opened his eyes to meet an awestruck Veronica.

CHAPTER 13

CHARLIE ROLAND SAT IN HIS office, with documents littering his desk. He simultaneously listened to the muffled sounds of the city and read and scanned through some of the documents. They were found and shipped to him in secret from Arabia. The documents were truly remarkable. Guadalupe Island and Greece both were showing an incredible indication that Raheem Gorroff wasn't the only one in the world to discover a strange paranormal object. As the president and founder of a company that thrived on weaponry and technology, he thought that these strange relics could be used as an endless power supply for America and her interests.

Roland possessed a somewhat cynical view of how a company should run. He secretly used fear tactics to get what he wanted out of buyers and did only what he thought was necessary to keep the ever-running motor of the company efficient. No one was powerful enough to stop him or his monopoly.

Roland Industries owned half the world's self-defense systems and government-related companies, including parts of the CIA,

NCIS, and the FBI. Government contractors thrived off of Roland's position. He was the holy money-giving maniac of the world if you were part of the military. He knew how to evade technicalities and create deals that no one could ever refuse. He was the perfect conman.

The Virginia Pilot had a selection where they ranked the highest and most powerful companies in the world along with their net worth. Disney was ranked fourth, coming in at $400 billion. Google was third, with $527 billion. Apple dominated them, with a total of $605 billion, and of course, Roland Industries came in first with an astronomical total of $708 billion. They were the first company in America to reach that amount. It made headlines with a heady combination of praise and backlash. People were outraged that a company of such magnitude was regarded so highly in the press, simply because they were strictly a weapons distribution center. However, after seven years of press conferences and meetings, the company was approved by the federal government to operate on the radar with no secrets kept from Charlie Roland and his newfound company.

As Roland pilfered through the files, he came across a file belonging to a woman named Jessica Santos. His mother's first name. He recalled a memory that he had often tried to eradicate from his past.

Charlie Roland found his talents in high school. He was always the shy kid who no one really understood. His mother, Jessica Roland, was an alcoholic and never paid him much attention as a child. The only thing she did for him was keep him in school. She even told him that after he was done with high school that she would kick him out and he was forced to live on his own. His father, Gerald, died when he was twelve, of stomach cancer. Charlie was absolutely devastated. The one man who inspired him to persevere and never quit had been ripped away from him at such a young age.

As soon as Charlie stepped off the bus, he could hear his mother screaming at him.

"Get in here! I told you to do the dishes before you left!" she hollered.

"I'm sorry, Mom. It won't happen again! I almost missed the bus. I didn't have time."

"Your father would be so ashamed of you! Maybe if you weren't so careless, your father would still be here," she slurred.

He waited that night until she passed out in the living room. He grabbed his father's snub-nose pistol, loaded it with a singular bullet, and shot her directly through her skull. Acting quickly, he dismantled the pistol and disposed of the parts in the nearby river.

He then called the police.

"Hello, 9-1-1, what's your—"

"Help! A man just broke into my house! I think he shot my mother," Charlie sobbed over the phone.

"Okay, just tell me your address, hun, and someone will be right over," the operator replied calmly. He recited his address between sobs, hung up, grabbed a bat, ran outside, and shattered the glass window in.

No one would have believed that such a small child would be capable of such a heinous crime. Later, he was transferred by child protective services to a foster home and was eventually adopted by a man named Alan Braxton, the CEO of Braxton Industries. Back then, they were a small weapons development division who assisted the air force for twenty years before filing for bankruptcy in the late nineties. Roland became proficient in both business and entrepreneurship under Braxton's wing. After nine more years, Roland had finally realized his calling, and he opened a business that ultimately reshaped the globe.

He concentrated on the rest of the text that wasn't blacked out as he formulated a plan. He leaned over and dialed a number, speaking the instant that the other line picked up.

"I need the CIA, please," he said.

"Yes, I'll hold." He sat in silence once more. "Hello, this is Charlie Roland. I need access to files dating back to December 4th, 1923.

Perfect, I expect a full detailed report on my desk tomorrow at two thirty p.m. Thank you very much." He hung up the phone.

Soon he would have all the files of every relic known to the government.

★ ★ ★

Lincoln laid on his hospital bed, left to wander subconsciously through his dreams. He dreamed of his daughter for the first time in years. Her smile spoke a thousand words of encouragement and happiness. She was truly both a gift and angel from God himself.

The sun was gleaming in the sky above. No clouds could be visible for as long as the eyes could see; it was just blue, and the one lonely star that beamed vibrant rays of warmth to the farmland below. Lincoln was taking his daughter for a drive through their farmlands that surrounded their rural hometown. The sun was setting with the grass looking alive as ever in the heart of summer. The trail of dust emanated from the ground below as the truck raced through the dusty road. Cornfields seemed as if they were never ending.

"Daddy, why do you have to leave again?" Patty asked.

"Because Daddy has a mission. He has to protect our country. Especially you."

Huffing in annoyance, she pouted. "But Daddy, then we can't watch Blue's Clues *together!" she said.*

"I know, honey, but when they tell me to go, I gotta go to save people from getting hurt. That's what it means to serve your country."

"When you come back, can we?"

"Yes, that sounds perfect. I'll be looking forward to it the whole time I'm gone," he said with a smile.

The dusty smell of the cornfields filled their noses, and he felt the crunching of gravel beneath the tires.

Abruptly, Lincoln's heart sank as black storm clouds appeared from nowhere. Rain stared to pour, and the radio shut off. Panic filled his chest, and he lost control of the truck. Mud and gravel cascaded along the road as the wheels skidded and the truck crashed into a tree.

Lincoln turned to see Patty run out of the truck to the other side to help him out. As soon as the pair touched hands, the wind increased, and she was swept off of her feet. The same swirling orb that took away his daughter reappeared. Lincoln held onto her hands for dear life as she screamed in fear.

"Daddy, help!" Patty screamed as her grip started to loosen. Lincoln's heart raced.

"Don't look at it, honey. Just look at me!" he cried.

Inevitably, Patty's small hands slipped from his grasp as she was sucked into the swirling blue light. He turned around just in time to see his truck flying toward him.

"No!" Lincoln screamed, sitting upright in bed.

He heard the sound of footsteps coming nearer. Thinking it could be the Spector, he tried to activate his electrodes. But all he could hear was a swirling, fizzing sound. He had completely forgotten he had destroyed the electrodes trying to kill Gorroff. Veronica ran into the room and saw Lincoln shaking violently with tears streaming down his face.

"Stay away!" he screamed in desperation.

Veronica was heartbroken that Gorroff had caused so much pain and hardship for Thaw. She ran to him and grabbed hold of his shoulders.

"Lincoln, stop! It's me, Veronica! Please stop!" she yelled.

He tensed his hand and mustered every ounce of energy he had. He whipped his hand through the air, and it came into contact with her left cheek. Surprisingly, she didn't respond angrily. She knew that whatever psychological state he was in, he had to be knocked out of it ASAP. She tensed her entire forearm. In one swift motion, she slapped him so hard his pupils dilated back to normal. He blinked a few times and stopped when he spotted a bruise on Veronica's cheek.

"I had another episode, didn't I?" Thaw asked.

This was a huge problem for Lincoln ever since Patty disappeared. He would remember waking up in the middle of the night, screaming and begging for Patty to come home. He would wake up the next morning still feeling as if a piece of his heart was gone. No medicine in the world could take that pain away.

"Veronica, I-I'm so sorry. I haven't dreamed of her in years. For the first time in years, I felt the ungodly loss. I can't have that back in my life again! I just can't!"

In that moment, an anxiety attack overcame him. His lungs felt as if they were going to collapse. He struggled to think straight while his hands shook. Immediately, Veronica grabbed a towel and ran to the nearest sink, saturating it with cold water. She tilted his head upward and tucked the towel underneath his neck to calm him down.

Success. He finally took a few breaths, and she put a hand to his chest to feel his heart. He was calming down. His body still shook violently from his nightmare and anxiety. She couldn't do anything more for him. After three minutes of her making him drink cold water and breathe slowly, Lincoln finally regained himself and turned his head to Veronica. She dabbed a cold towel on his forehead as he stared at her.

"What a mess," he said, closing his eyes.

"You're not the only one with problems, you know," Veronica said.

"I'm sorry," Lincoln said. "Were you given a super suit that magnifies your limbs and kicks twice as much ass? No, I didn't think so."

"Give me any more sass and I'll hit you again," Veronica said. "So how's the superhero life treating ya?"

Lincoln rolled his eyes. "I'm no hero, just trying to get shit done in a mad world with teleporting terrorists. You know, the usual," he said. "Thank you for all you did. I feel awful you were thrown into this."

"You've been a friend of mine for so long I've forgotten what it's like not to know you. Doing this for you is nothing big at all. I would do anything for a friend."

"You know, in all my years of getting shot at and blown up, I always wondered how you kept on going with what happened to Ben."

"Ben has that special touch to him that makes me happy inside. When Ben came home with his legs disabled, I did everything for him because I knew that later down the road, he would get better and return the favor to someone else. He can look death in the face and smile. He may not look like it at times, but he's a fighter. Just like the kids."

"When this is done, I promise you Ben will get better and I'll never have to put this suit on again."

"Somehow, I don't think you're ever going to give up that suit of yours," she said, poking him in the chest.

"Technically, it's Adam's," Lincoln said, correcting her. "Wait, what about the sword?" he asked in a panic. "What's the status of that?"

"Two things. One, you're not going anywhere yet. And two, it's still being examined."

"I gotta get up and help them. I'm tired of being in this bed."

He rose on his haunches, but she pressed her hand on his chest to hold him down.

"Lincoln Joseph Thaw, so help me God, I will hit you again," Veronica said.

"That was rude," he joked.

"I know," Veronica responded.

Thomas and Adam stood in the lab staring at the captured relic. They studied every nanometer of the golden blade that rested before them. Wires were connected to the hilt and blade. Screens were everywhere, dominating the walls. No anomaly was getting past Adam and Thomas.

"The sword seems to be self-sustaining its own reserved power supply somehow," Adam observed as he gazed upon a computer screen that relayed to him different information.

"What do you mean, reserved power? That makes no sense. The last time someone tampered with this thing, people died," Thomas replied.

"Let me remind you, Mr. Lunardi, that they were using what is now primitive analysis technology to process it," Adam said. "I have the latest cutting-edge technology. I assure you that there is nothing to fear here."

"That's what worries me," Thomas said. He locked his eyes on the blade. "Do we know where it even gets its power from?"

"From what the scanners have been reading, its power is massive, but it fluctuates from time to time. It's incredibly odd, and it is unknown as to where it comes from," Adam said.

He walked over to a chair with a bowl-like shape mounted where the head would be. It was connected to Excalibur via the wires. At least fifty cords were clipped onto the blade and connected to the bowl structure.

"Exactly what the hell is that?" Thomas asked.

"This is an Internal Neurological Brainwave Easer. I developed it a long time ago to help with patients that mostly suffer from PTSD. But I never got the chance to actually test it out. I guess now's the best time to try it." Adam flipped switches and pressed buttons on the back of the chair.

"You've never tested it out? Not only that, but you're connecting it to something that may explode?"

"That surface is reinforced and enhanced with construction glass. Nothing will be able to get in or out. Believe me, we'll be okay. Besides, nobody knew that it was going to spontaneously explode the first time."

"What do you want me to do while you're connected to that thing?" Thomas asked.

Adam looked up from the switches and smiled.

"I'm not going to be connected to it. You are," he responded slowly. Thomas felt his blood run cold.

"Hold it. Hold it now! Wait a minute, I never agreed to this! What if that thing fries my brain?"

"The most you'll feel is a little prick of electricity once the machine is activated. From there, your brain will work as a sponge, soaking in every ounce of information Excalibur has to offer."

"Adam. Sponges have holes in them. You're sure this will work?" Thomas asked reluctantly.

"Completely."

"Then count me in," Thomas said reluctantly.

Adam was pleasantly surprised he agreed to his terms. Nevertheless, Thomas sat in the chair, and the bowl was lowered and strapped to his head. It felt as if he was in an electric chair. The humming of machines grew louder with each passing second. The lights in the room seemed to dim due to the high voltage this thing was using. Thomas kept his eyes transfixed on the ground and spoke in a low voice.

"I'm scared shitless, Adam. I have no idea what to expect here. What if I end up dying from this?" Thomas asked. Adam put his hands on his knees and bent down slowly to face him on his level.

"If something does come up, then I can shut the system down. I'm going to ask this once, Thomas. Are you ready?"

Thomas closed his eyes and took a deep breath. He wondered if this was the last time he'd ever be conscious again. His mind raced, but he took another breath to calm down. He slowly opened his eyes and titled his head upward to look at Adam.

"I'm ready. Fire it up," Thomas said.

Adam nodded and walked around to the back of the chair. A large yellow lever was positioned upright. He grabbed hold of the lever and just held it. He was hesitant because he too was scared of the outcome. This would be the first time he would actually try this invention, in addition to changing the internal mechanics. Adam did the calculations himself and discovered that the chances of Thomas getting irrevocably injured were at a terrifying 78.8 percent. Thomas closed his eyes and waited. He slowly counted to twenty.

"One . . . I can do this . . . "

"Two . . . I can do this . . . "

"Three . . . for Veronica."

"Four . . . for Lincoln."

"Five . . . for Adam."

"Six . . . for . . . "

Suddenly, he heard a *cling* of a lever and felt a moderate shock in his brain. He closed his eyes and froze.

CHAPTER 14

ALL THOMAS COULD SEE WAS the vastness of space rushing toward him. The mirage of fast-approaching planets soared around him. His body felt weightless as he thrashed around. His vision grew blurry, and he tried to remember what exactly he was doing in this place. Frantic thoughts and emotions overwhelmed him. He screamed as the endless void grew faster. Suddenly, everything went black.

What is this? Where am I? Thomas thought.

He looked around to find himself in an empty black nothingness. No matter where he looked and turned, there was no life, no sign of hope, and no sign of anything that could help him. Thomas's heart raced as he called out to Adam, but there was no response. Suddenly, a bright flash appeared, and he shielded his eyes.

Before him were gigantic orbs that held galaxies upon universes. Above and below, from left to right, and as vast as the eyes could see, there were countless orbs of bioluminescent light. Stars surrounded him, forming numerous galaxies and clusters of stars that floated about. He was now peacefully drifting amongst an invisible current that only space could manifest.

A yellow orb appeared directly before him. It was strangely mesmerizing. However, to his amazement, it started to change and grow sleek, slender limbs until a beautiful woman floated right in front of him, gazing into his eyes. Thomas was speechless. The woman's face was a conglomerate of stars. She was the epitome of beauty, and her blue hair drifted in the non-existent atmosphere.

"Welcome, Thomas Wade Lunardi. I've been awaiting your arrival," the majestic woman said.

Thomas struggled to come up with words to respond.

"You are in what is known as the Multi-Precinct, a place beyond the fabric of time and reality. My name is Aura, and I am the guardian of life itself," she stated.

"Are you God?" Thomas asked.

"I am not God. However, I hold many of the traits the Almighty possesses. I see all. I'm in all, and I protect all who value life."

"Aura, what a pretty name. I once knew a girl named—"

"Your puny attempt to further escalate our acquaintance is amusing. In addition, you have never met another woman who has had the same name as me. I know you very well, Lunardi. Better than you know your inner subconscious."

"Lady, you don't know a single damn thing about me. Cut to the chase, and tell me where Excalibur came from already."

"Sadly, your tactics will have no effect on me. I'm above such things. You're not the only human being to try and inflict this technique on me. It is quite amazing that humans express increased aggression to achieve answers when all they must do is simply ask. War is such a savage procedure. It tears apart the life force that is bestowed inside those involved."

"Gee, doesn't that make me feel just dandy?"

"I did not mean to offend. All I stated was that you are a part of a race that I have observed before the first man invented the wheel. Everything falls into place perfectly. Life and death must exist in balance: one cannot exist without the other."

"You're still not answering my question."

"Oh, but I am, Mr. Lunardi. Your world is so quick to simplify and dispose any impossibilities when, in actuality, such things are possible through belief in the unlikely. For example, Excalibur the golden blade that has been the source of legend for generations . . . "

This piqued Thomas's attention. She knew where the sword came from, and he was determined to find out where.

"I have already glimpsed a few seconds into the future. It is clear you would like to ask me from where the sword originated," Aura said.

She neither moved her limbs while she spoke nor wore a frown. She was something else. Something that defied everything humans knew about the universe.

"You are a very interesting human being, Lunardi. You come from a family with the misfortunes of poverty, death, and miscommunication. You joined the American military to make a difference in your imperfect world. You have accomplished your life's goal, yet you continue to torment your soul through military service. Why do you feel this is necessary?"

"Because bad people exist and they gotta know American diplomacy is better than communism and tyranny. Which brings us to Gorroff."

"You are only the third human from your reality to enter into this Precinct. Hakim and Raheem Gorroff have both been here, but one of them had too much evil coursing within the confines of their subconscious."

"I've dealt with those two before. They're both terrorists, for Christ's sake! You're telling me that one of them isn't evil to the core?"

"I sent Hakim to a place where he can start anew."

"You let a monster get away from you?!"

"I saw deeply hidden potential within him. When one can look deep inside the confines of the human brain, one would be absolutely astounded at the mystery it contains. All because one has done and executed countless acts of injustice in the past does not automatically mean they are condemned for the rest of their ethereal existence."

"Look, Aura. You can't just let people like that get by you. It doesn't matter if he was willing to reform. He was still a terrorist, and his type don't just change! He murdered God only knows how many people."

"Two hundred seventy-six American soldiers and thirty-four of his own soldiers. However, I can see trillions of light years into the future. I can see a group of quadruplet stars form at one time and slowly emanate light amongst void of space time. If I can see occurrences that regular eyes could not see, don't you think that I can see within the human soul?"

Thomas was taken aback. She was right. Every word out of her mouth was the truth. He swallowed his pride and took a deep breath.

"Please," Thomas started, "if you won't tell me where Excalibur came from, then how do we stop the Golden Spector?"

"Watch the blade and protect it. Should evil arise and take control, look for the place which holds the scroll."

Everything around them started to appear as if they were going light speed through deep space. The stars and planets that surrounded Thomas rushed past him, and his head started to feel dizzy, as if he was waking up from a dream. Thomas opened his eyes to see Adam screaming into his face with Lincoln and Veronica standing in the background. Everything was blurry, and his voice sounded muffled. "Thomas! Thomas! Wake up! I said wake up!" Adam yelled.

"I'm awake, goddamn it! Stop yelling at me!"

"What happened, Thomas?" Adam asked.

"I don't know," Thomas said. "But I sure as hell know what to do about the Spector."

"Suddenly, you know what you're talking about?" Lincoln teased.

"Lincoln, you don't understand what I saw."

"What did you find out about the sword?" Adam asked.

"Nothing," he said. "But there was someone else . . . a woman. Her name was Aura. She was so . . . stunningly gorgeous. She called herself the guardian of a place called the . . . Multi-Precinct? She said she had been in existence since forever."

Veronica was shocked, as was Adam.

"Where is this place?" Adam asked.

"Somewhere far, far away from here, man. Somewhere that defies everything we know. I never want to go there ever again. Just get me out of this thing."

Adam unlatched the arm and leg restraints. He took a breath and looked around.

"Damn, it feels good to be back. Not having gravity is weird," Thomas said.

"It's good to have you back, man," Lincoln said, hugging him.

"I'm so happy you're alive and safe," Veronica said, hugging Thomas as well.

"You guys are acting like I was dead or something," Thomas stated.

"Because you were dead," Lincoln said. "You died for about a solid two minutes before Adam revived your heart. You were gone."

Thomas's jaw dropped. "I was dead? I'm sure it wasn't that bad, was it?"

Lincoln walked over to the computer that recorded Thomas's brainwaves while he was asleep and pulled up an image that confirmed his claim.

"You died, man. You flat lined," he said.

"Well, what can I say? That was the best two minutes and forty-two seconds of sleep I've had in my entire life."

"You never answered Adam's question," Veronica said. "Did you ever find out where the sword came from?"

"The woman said something along the lines of: watch the blade with protection intent. Should evil arise and take control, look for the place which holds the scroll."

Before they had a chance to respond, a call could be heard from the overhead intercom.

"Emergency Alert! Emergency Alert!" said the automated voice echoing through the overhead speakers. Adam, Thomas, Veronica, and Lincoln hurried out into the hallway and ran to the main computer room, where they found the main screen buzzing and recording numerical data streams.

"What's the problem?" Lincoln asked.

"Seems like Roland Industries satellite systems picked up a strange anomaly in the mountains near England. It's registering radioactivity in that area. The readings from this thing are off the chart. I can pinpoint exactly where it is in a matter of minutes."

"Do you think . . . ?" Thomas started to ask.

"The scroll? In England?" Veronica asked.

"But wait, why would the scroll be radioactive?" asked Lincoln.

"Regardless of whether this is the scroll or not, it's our job to investigate anything with readings this high," Adam replied.

"Adam, how fast can we get that suit fixed and ready to go?" Lincoln asked.

"With every computer in this facility on my side? Three hours at the max," Adam said.

"Looks like I'm going to England to check it out before anyone else gets there. At least Raheem won't be a threat anymore," Lincoln said.

★ ★ ★

Raheem floated lifelessly in the river. The bullet hole in his head oozed blood that trickled into the water around him.

An unsuspecting man approached the river with a fishing pole and tackle box. He took his sandals off to better feel the sandy dirt beneath him and attached a worm to the hook of his pole. He cocked his arm and cast into the water with a light plop. The black water camouflaged the blood that drifted only a few feet away.

The bullet hole miraculously healed. Raheem's body twitched wildly, and the strength returned to his limbs. His usual shredded clothes now morphed into the globally known golden alloy and glistened in the blackness. A golden halo appeared over his body and worked its way slowly down his head and shoulders.

He felt different. Instead of feeling blood pumping through his veins, he felt incomparable power. His heart surged with vengeance and rage, a very devastating combination.

Prepare yourself, Marksman. The trophy will be mine once more. Your friends will choke to death by my hands, and I will impale your chest with Excalibur. Once you're gone, the world will be mine for the taking, and the scroll will unlock the secrets of the sword, Raheem thought.

His senses were now fully heightened to their maximum limit. He cocked his head upward and bent his legs. He thrusted himself from the murky lake. He stopped right in front of the worm on the hook and grabbed it, squeezing it. With one swift motion, he yanked on the wire, and the man above holding the fishing line was pulled through the air and into the water. Before the man could swim back to the shore, he felt a hand on his ankle. His heart skipped a beat as he felt another hand grab his other ankle. The man was pulled under the surface in a matter of seconds. Water filled his eyes and lungs. He struggled against a force he could not see. He thrashed his arms to swim back to the surface but was pulled deeper. When the bubbles disappeared and everything became visible, the man rested his eyes on the terrifying sight of Raheem smiling manically at him. The man screamed under the water, air bubbles escaping from his mouth.

The man's skin progressively grew pale. The color in his eyes faded as his body aged and deteriorated. In a matter of seconds, his body turned to dust and swirled in the water's indifferent current, leaving his clothes to drift in the water.

Raheem's eyes were now blood red as his body became stronger with every passing second. He cocked his head to the surface above and rocketed himself out of the deep, dark abyss.

"I see that you have not yet achieved your task, Mr. Gorroff,"

Aura's voice reverberated through his skull. *"Time is stretching thin in your world. I'd advise you not to take Excalibur."*

"I have been dead for almost two full days! Why shouldn't I take what is rightfully mine?"

"I see your powers have manifested onto you already. Mr. Thaw is on his way to England along with his closest ally, Thomas. They plan to return Excalibur to its rightful place of origin. There you must meet them and read the scroll to reset the spell that Excalibur is under. Join them in their quest for saving humanity. If one of you does not read the scroll, then the planet as you know it will cease to exist and cause a chain reaction that will destroy a parallel four hundred eighty-seven thousand Earths. Do not disappoint me, Raheem. This is your final opportunity for redemption . . . "

He laughed. The earth deserved utter destruction. His whole life, he knew what it was like to be tossed aside, mentally tortured, abused, and used as a war propaganda tool. This was his time to show everyone what he was made of.

"Lincoln Thaw, your heart will be underneath my boot, and this world will end by my hand," Raheem vowed.

CHAPTER 15

THE SUIT WAS READY AND the plan set. Adam applied the finishing touches to Lincoln's defense weapon system.

Adam spent the last hour applying an additional battle suit for Thomas. This battle suit was smuggled from Roland Industries and hidden in Adam's office just in case someone broke in and threatened his life. The weapon was a standard battle suit: all black with a zipper running along the wearer's spine. The pants were black with two pistol holsters on each thigh. Grey boots were also standardized additions to every employee of Roland Industries. However, this suit had modifications that Adam invented.

For instance, the boots had built-in shock absorbers that could make a kick lethal in any predicament. The pistols were equipped with cement-piercing bullets that could cut through just about anything. The jacket was created using the same memory metal alloy as Thaw's suit. A singular chip was at the back of Thomas's right ear that acted as a holographic helmet. This technology solidified once the electrons in the molecules were activated. All he had to do was tap the chip and his face could be sealed off from the elements and enemy fire. Thomas zipped the jacket up, savoring the moment.

"You know, Thaw? Now I know the feeling of being a badass in shining armor like you," he said.

"You may talk the talk, but can you walk the walk?" Lincoln asked.

"Watch yourself, Thaw. Were you the one to go to the Multi-Precinct? I don't think so," Thomas retorted.

"Okay, smartass. Just don't get us killed, all right?"

"I died for too minutes and I'm fine—" Thomas joked.

Veronica rushed into the training room where Thomas and Lincoln stood ready.

"I've made up my mind, guys," Veronica said. "I'm not staying here with Adam. No way. I'm going to the hospital to stay with Ben and the kids. If something happens, I need to be with them. I know you guys will kick some serious ass."

"After she's transported to the hospital, you two are gonna be teleported to Great Britain," Adam said. "I've pinpointed the exact coordinates that gave off the radioactive ions. All you have to do is find the scroll and let me know so I can teleport you back home and end this nightmare. Radio me as soon as you get your hands on that artifact. Your earpieces should be fully operational, so staying in contact won't be hard."

Lincoln and Thomas tapped the earpieces, and a small voice could be heard.

"Roland Bluetooth connection online."

"Whatever happens, please let me know," Veronica said. "I sure as hell don't want to be the last person to know what happens to you."

She walked up to Thomas first and hugged him tightly. He returned the favor and embraced her in his arms. She let go from him and walked over to Lincoln. Deep down, she knew this might be the last time she would ever see them.

"Veronica, are you okay?" he asked her calmly. She moved her head to look at him, and her face was completely pale. Tears streamed down her face. She struggled for words.

"Of course I'm not! But I swear to God, Lincoln, if you die in this mess, then who's Ben gonna go fishing with? Why is it we can't live a normal life? I don't want you two to die."

"You don't have to worry about us dying," Lincoln said. "We've been through worse. I swear to you, Veronica Frost, I will come back alive. We've lost too much to turn back now."

She let go of him and walked over to Adam. "I'm ready," she said.

Adam reached into his pocket and took out a small pin, applying it to Veronica's shirt. He then tapped the middle of it, and it started to flash green. It flashed faster until her body phased away like an apparition.

"Adam, take us away," Lincoln said.

He walked over to Lincoln and attached another pin to his chest. He could feel it sucking onto his skin and suddenly felt a tingling sensation flowing through his entire body. He watched as his hands slowly dissipated into nothingness.

As far as Lincoln knew, the trip was instantaneous. He expected to see a blinding flash of light, but he was instantly transported into the middle of a wooded area with nothing but green grass and abundant trees as far as the eyes could see. Dappled sunlight streamed through the leaves and branches with the breeze brushing against them. He heard a faint whistling noise behind him and noticed Thomas morphing into existence a few feet away.

"Damn, that was fast," Thomas said as he paced about, making sure his legs still worked. The wind then picked up and knocked him over, causing him to fall into the grass. Lincoln walked over and offered him a hand, which he accepted.

"Are you drunk or just a light weight?" Lincoln asked.

"Ha, so funny," Thomas retorted, glaring at him. "Remind me where we're supposed to go again?"

Lincoln lifted his right arm and activated his onboard holographic projection database. A rectangle appeared in the air before him as he tapped the icons and keyboards. Finally, a red blinking light appeared on a radar-like screen.

"We go north," Lincoln said. "If we're lucky, we won't run into anyone. My radar is clean, but be on your guard. At this point, nothing would surprise me." Thomas reached into his gun holsters and whipped them out, ready for anything.

The pair continued along the winding green trail, which held parallel trees beside them. Five minutes became twenty, stretched to thirty, and eventually turned into an hour. Thomas was growing impatient.

"Lincoln, if I go another foot, my legs are going to give out again," he said. He put his pistols back into their holsters. There was no point in having them out.

The sun seemed to laugh at them as they reached a clearing. Lincoln kept his eyes glued to the holographic projection that guided them on his arm. Lincoln and Thomas were now in a wide-open grassy area with the breeze creating waves through the grass. The air around them was serene. Something didn't seem right.

"Lincoln, something's off," Thomas said, taking the guns back out. He looked around and held them up. Lincoln's eyes darted from side to side, scanning everything in their surroundings.

"My radar isn't picking up anything except the signal we've been tracking. Keep your guard up and stay behind me. I know we're close. We have to be," Lincoln said.

The pair continued to trudge upward over the hill until they reached the peak. Before them was a small town below that rested next to a large lake. A small farm was at the adjacent side of the village, with cows lumbering around their small confined pastures. A gargantuan mountain stood behind the small town, almost overlooking it as if it were a silent protector.

"Zoom in," Lincoln told the computer inside his mask.

His eyesight was magnified, allowing him to see a black cave embedded in the center of the mountain. The automated targeting system confirmed it. In that mountain was their target. Getting there would take a couple additional hours. Lincoln did not want to waste any time at all.

"Why couldn't Adam have transported us closer to the mountain? What a dick," Thomas said.

"Maybe his pins are still in the prototype stage. Be glad we got here in one piece," Lincoln responded.

"I have an idea to get there, but it's going to be risky. With the right trajectory, we can transport ourselves using your blasters on the highest setting. Wish we still had Adam's instant teleporters. Each pistol for each person. It's a stretch, but if it works, then we can get the scroll a lot faster."

Thomas looked at him like he was crazy.

"I'm sorry, you want us to what? You've had some pretty god-awful ideas in the past, but this one takes the cake. A pistol can't launch you off the ground, Thaw! It's impossible! If we miscalculate where we blast off, then we could smack into the mountain and fall to our deaths! Hell no!" Thomas exclaimed.

"You got any better suggestions? We need to try it. Trust me."

Thomas looked over at the mountain looming in the distance.

"You know, man, I love you, but your crazy-ass ideas need to stop. I don't know how we keep finding each other in these scenarios, but screw it. I'm in."

He reached into his holsters and withdrew his guns. He handed Lincoln one of the pistols.

"Set yours to the highest blaster setting," Lincoln instructed.

Thomas twisted the muzzle counterclockwise until he heard a faint *click*. A slow humming sound emanated from the gun, letting Thomas know that the blaster setting was combat-ready. The gun idled with its humming.

"What now, boss?" Thomas asked.

Lincoln looked over the vast scenery. He concentrated for a

moment, and his vision became filled with trajectory calculations and every possible outcome. Suddenly, a voice recording sounded in his ears.

"Hello, Mr. Thaw," said the voice. "*I have had my team develop a microchip in your earpiece that analyzes your coordinated attack patterns and calculates your best alternatives when in combat. The chip is fused with the memory metal's donor's system every time they are near a close radius of one another. Good luck, Mr. Thaw.*"

Lincoln knew the voice belonged to Mr. Roland. But why would his voice be programmed to go off when the software was activated? Under normal circumstances, it would be Adam's voice.

"All right, let's get this started," Lincoln said to himself as he watched the computer in his mask calculate every possible way he could catapult himself. The mask displayed a red line pointing from the hilltop they rested on.

Destination Approximation: 87.9%
Rendered Calculated Survival Rate: 67.7%
Wind Resistance: 56.4%
Overall Possibility of Survival: 54.6%

Lincoln cringed. "Thaw, what's the game plan?" Thomas asked.

Lincoln didn't know what to say. He didn't want to answer the exact number because it would only prove Thomas's point about the danger level.

"We have a good chance of getting over there," Lincoln said as the rendered simulation in his mask evaporated. "If we leave now, we can get back with time to spare. Let's position ourselves and get ready." Deep down, Lincoln was terrified of heights. He kept it to himself. He was trained for hand-to-hand combat, but due to recent events, he was rapidly rising in rank with the difficulty of these missions.

"All right, Thomas, listen. We're gonna angle ourselves in a crouching position and point the blasters to the ground at a forty-five-degree angle. Once you've hit the air then try to angle yourself with the cave. If this fails, pull the parachute on the back of your suit so you can land safely. I'll be right beside you."

Thomas looked at Lincoln with terrified eyes. "It's okay, you got this. You've always had it," Lincoln said.

Thomas angled himself and bent his knees, feeling the stress in his legs. He sat for an additional thirty seconds before working up the nerve to pull the trigger to the blaster. He could feel the wind flowing and hitting his hair, almost telling him that everything was going to be all right. His heart beat quickened, and he broke into a sweat as his anxiety increased. He closed his eyes and concentrated. He decided he was going to count to three and blast off.

"One . . . " he started as he crouched even further down. He pointed the gun to the grass behind him and took a few deep breaths. Lincoln did the same.

"Two . . . " he continued as his grip on the trigger tightened. He squeezed his eyes shut, not wanting to see what was going to happen next.

"Three . . . " he said as he pulled the trigger and heard a blast that obliterated the ground.

Lincoln shielded himself with his arms from the dirt and soil that polluted the air. When the dust settled, he was gone. Lincoln whipped his head around to the sky above and watched Thomas fly through the air, screaming.

All Thomas could see was the grassy plain below him. The mountain was approaching faster than he expected. The sound of the wind rushing through his ears was all he could hear. His knuckles turned white holding onto the blaster for dear life. Thomas angled his body as Lincoln instructed so that he was positioned downward to land in the cave's threshold. The clouds raced past him as he tried his hardest focus on landing one of the craziest stunts of his career.

The cave was now in arm's length; he braced himself for impact and deployed his parachute in a panic. Suddenly, an updraft pushed the parachute off course. Thomas spiraled out of control and hit the rocky terrain of the mountainside.

The string connecting him to the parachute snapped, and Thomas clung to the face of the mountain, his heart racing with adrenaline. The suit he wore shielded him from the elements, and none of his bones were broken, as far as he knew. Thomas didn't dare look down from the precipice. He gritted his teeth and attempted to maneuver himself downward to the cave's opening. Gradually, he found his boot in empty black space. He dropped downward and landed on the hard gravel of the cave entrance. To his surprise, he spotted a familiar figure in the shadows.

"Somehow, I knew you'd be here," Thomas said as he activated the pistol.

Without hesitation, Lincoln pulled the trigger and quickly felt the propulsion carry him toward the cave. Unlike Thomas, Lincoln had a mask on, so he could see well despite the wind rushing all around him. The computer system in the mask showed numerous different calculations flashing on the screen, allowing him to see everything that was happening all around him. The ground below was far and distant, almost worlds away.

His breathing increased, and his fear grew. He watched as the cave drew nearer and closer with each passing second. He was almost there. All it took was a couple more seconds.

Meanwhile, back in Roland Industries, Charlie Roland watched through the spy-cam embedded in the eyes of Lincoln's mask. He sat in his chair watching the monitor within his glass desk. He rubbed his hands together. He couldn't believe that Adam would attempt to steal this level of tech without realizing there were countermeasures installed. When Adam first got the job at Roland Industries, he had potential. Roland then put him to the test by asking him for better-developed security cameras to install in the facility. He succeeded by installing thirty separate cameras in an orb that moved around every minute of every day, recording everything in a close proximity.

"Oh dear, Mr. Thaw, what are you up to?" he asked himself.

He watched the monitor intently, waiting for Thaw to discover the artifact he so desired. "Mr. Thaw, you're too generous. You're doing all the work for me," Roland muttered.

★ ★ ★

Lincoln soared through the air approaching the cave but suddenly realized that his course was shifted to the left. His body spiraled out of control. Suddenly he remembered his blades. He drew them a split second before he hit the rock face, driving them deep into the granite. He pressed hidden buttons located on his arm. They activated, making a loud, metallic slicing sound; they were primed in the case of any possible attack. The cave was now about twenty feet to his right. He flung out his right arm, making contact with the rock gouging a vein of sediment. He gradually traversed laterally toward the cave. The sound of crunching rock and sediment echoed through the ravine with pieces of rock falling to the ground far below.

With one final lurch, Lincoln stepped into the entryway of the cave.

His strength was the only thing he had left to extricate himself and capture the scroll.

Lincoln pulled off his gloves to feel the air around them once again. He had all the luck in the world not to be dead. He clenched his fists to feel them once again and flexed them around a little before sliding them back on. He was bound and determined to finish this mission and go home. However, the question remained: *where was Thomas?*

He began to take off but stopped at the sight of the cave before him. There was nowhere else to go except into the depths of the cave. He surveyed his surroundings. He appeared to be in some kind of medieval temple. Lanterns were shining everywhere while artistic depictions of knights littered the aged ceiling tiles above. He looked down and saw a glorious image of Excalibur emblazoned the ground. Lincoln suddenly realized that this had to be the place where the scroll was concealed.

It's here. I know it's here. It has to be, he thought as his gaze fell upon the ritualized skeletons embedded in the chiseled walls. Then a voice called out.

"Buddy, get me out of here!" he heard Thomas yell. Lincoln snapped his head back, looked in the other direction, and glared.

I guess it was just a matter of time before you showed up to get the scroll," Lincoln said.

CHAPTER 16

THE GOLDEN SPECTOR SAT IN a beaten, broken-down throne. In one hand, he held Excalibur, the tip touching the floor. In the other hand, he restrained a battered-looking Thomas by the throat. He was choking on his own blood.

"Oh, how I've missed you, Mr. Thaw. You thought that a mortal woman's shot could kill me? Let me tell you something about death. It's the most riveting experience I've ever felt," Raheem said.

"Maybe if you stayed dead then you would have felt even better," Lincoln responded. "How do you know who I am?"

"Isn't it a little obvious after obliterating the base in Norfolk? All those papers flying around with your name on them?"

"I don't care if you know who I am. Let Thomas go and put down the sword so we can fight like men. It's me you want!"

"Hey, Thaw," Thomas said between gasps of air. Lincoln turned to look at him. "Kick his ass for me," he spat out before Raheem shoved Excalibur through Thomas's leg, leaving him pinned to the ground. He screamed in utter agony. His blood gushed out of his leg.

Raheem smiled and turned to Lincoln, expecting fear. Instead, he was greeted by a blunt and painful punch to the face. Lincoln punched him repeatedly in the eyes, nose, and ears. He finished his assault by lifting him over his head and throwing him forcefully to the ground. Then Lincoln ran to his wounded comrade in an attempt to help him, but an unnatural force enveloped his body. A fluctuating beam shot out of Raheem's hands.

With adrenaline pumping, Lincoln jumped up from the ground and ran to Thomas once more until he was hit by another beam. This time, it was twice as powerful. He hit the wall with such a force that the rock behind him cracked on impact. Raheem hit him with yet another beam from his other hand and began walking toward him, making the pressure almost unbearable. Thomas watched with tears of pain streaming down his face. He could do nothing but watch as his friend was senselessly beaten.

★ ★ ★

Charlie Roland watched the events unfolding before him from the comfort of his office. He watched as Raheem stepped right in front of him, continuing to blast him with the endless stream of energy beams. The live feed was cut for Roland, and he slammed his fist on the glass in anger, shattering it. He closed his eyes and took a breath to calm himself before he did anything he would regret. Now nothing could be traced to him.

★ ★ ★

Lincoln ground his teeth in pain as he felt his whole body start to hum with the power flowing over him. His readouts were back along with his gadgets.

"*All Systems Back Online,*" the voice within his mask said.

"When I'm done killing you, I will take over this world. Your government will fail, your cities will be mine for the taking, and your pathetic friends will be resting comfortably under a gravestone!" Raheem declared maliciously.

"Yeah, good luck with that," he said as he activated a flash grenade hooked to his belt.

He flipped his thumb upward and pulled the pin, activating the explosive. He intentionally dropped it and rolled it over to Raheem's feet. He looked down and panicked. In a flash, Lincoln's eye protectors shielded his vision from the blinding light as it detonated. Raheem screamed as he closed his eyes, temporarily blinded by the grenade. Lincoln propelled himself from the ground and activated his Mini-Electrodes. He punched Raheem so hard that he went flying into the throne and cracked it on impact. He ran to Thomas, who was still pinned to the ground, grabbed the handle of the sword, and attempted to pull, but to no avail. Thomas screamed in anguish. Lincoln leaned down to look at his friend.

"Listen, I need you to focus on something else while I get this thing out of you, okay?" Lincoln asked. Thomas nodded and squeezed his eyes shut.

"Hold on, buddy. One way or another, this day's gonna end with that scroll in our hands," Lincoln reassured him. He grasped the handle once more and felt a surge of energy rush through him. Suddenly, a booming voice echoed throughout the temple.

"This Forgotten Temple Holds the Scroll. If ye be worthy shall have the soul,
Speak the Words that Free the Text, Let the World be Free, Not Next."

The walls seemed to shake as Lincoln froze in place, holding the sword. He gently started to pull the blade out of his comrade's leg. However, Thomas didn't utter a sound. As a matter of fact, the more he pulled the sword, Thomas's leg seemed to heal itself. Once the blade was fully out of his friend's leg, Thomas whipped his head back.

"I'll be damned. Did you just make that thing speak?" he asked, trying to get up.

"Guess I did. We have to find the scroll fast and ask questions later. Quick, go look around for anything that could be connected to the scroll," Lincoln said. Thomas took off running, darting his eyes in every direction, and saw Raheem get back up.

Raheem struggled to his feet. His wounds healed themselves, and the sounds of cracking bones emanated from his body. He finally stood, fully healed, and gazed upon Thomas running down a dark corridor that lead deeper into the unknown. He was about to follow him until he heard a voice call out to him.

"Raheem, I'm the one you want. Let's even the score already!" Lincoln shouted, holding the sword at his side. He clutched it tightly and felt the surge of power rushing through his veins.

"Shut up!" Raheem yelled as he levitated off the ground and engulfed his hands in golden spheres of light. His eyes dripped with scarlet energy. He screamed as he blasted both beams at him.

Lincoln flung the sword upward. He expected to be hit with the disastrous energy beam, but instead he felt nothing. He opened his eyes and discovered that the beam clashed with Excalibur.

Raheem stared in shock. He grew irate at the sight of their evenly matched power. He screamed as he added more pressure. Lincoln held onto the sword and closed his eyes.

Lincoln walked slowly toward Raheem and stopped right in front of him. Raheem ceased his beam of light and stared, confused. The sword glowed with expanding intensity until it blinded both men. Abruptly, a bright and powerful beam erupted from the sword. The blast was so immense that a few stalactites fell from the ceiling of the tomb. Raheem was sent flying through a wall.

"Come on out, you coward," Lincoln said.

"As you wish," he heard a voice say from beyond. Raheem teleported in front of him and yanked the sword from Lincoln's grasp before he vanished again.

"Activate the electrodes," he told the computer thorough his mask. He felt electricity surge through the gloves. A minute went by and there was nothing. Another minute, another minute, and then another. Nothing happened.

"Thomas, have you found anything? Thomas?" he asked, but the signal wasn't going through. There was no telling where he was at this point.

★★★

Thomas was standing in the middle of a small tomb that had Medieval Latin inscribed on the granite walls. He walked up to one of the inscriptions to discover a man dressed in black holding Excalibur generations after King Arthur wielded it. He continued his mission searching for the scroll. He looked everywhere but found only inscribed tablets and intricate, high relief sculptures adorning the walls. The only other company Thomas had was the singular ancient casket, which appeared as if it sat for thousands of years. Spiderwebs dominated the crevices and carvings. Thomas refused to approach something so ominous and primordial.

He leaned his head back and took a deep breath. He felt a brick he was leaning on behind him push inward, and the floor began to shake with dust flying into the air. The coffin that laid before him began to crack and break. He was afraid that the corpse inside would fall out and spill deathly remains onto the floor. He shielded his face with his arms and squeezed his eyes shut. Expecting to see a dead body lying on the floor, he was greeted instead by a supernatural sight.

"My God," he muttered under his breath.

A golden, wrapped piece of cloth tied shut by an ancient ribbon floated above the broken casket. Its essence was welcoming with whispers mysteriously echoing from it. He remembered what the voice said about reading the scroll and reading the text. Thomas's mind was filled with questions. He was instantly compelled to take the scroll and receive whatever knowledge it possessed.

He walked cautiously over to the scroll and extended his hand to grasp it. His fingers touched the base of the scroll, and his mind began to flash images and memories that weren't his. All the memories seemed as if they were from a time long before his own. He saw knights dueling with Excalibur, kingdoms destroyed and built, and buried temples. The final flash he received was the sight of Lincoln holding Excalibur in his hand with a beam of light in the sky.

"It's like one thing after another around here, I swear," he said as he began to open the scroll.

But it wouldn't budge. Not a single inch. Suddenly, Thomas remembered what the quote said about the scroll. "*This Forgotten Temple Holds the Scroll. If ye be worthy shall have the soul.*" It made sense now. He obviously didn't have the soul to read or open the paper to see what was inside. But he could still take it to Lincoln and have him read it. He rushed to where the two opposing forces battled for the future for humanity.

"That sword belongs to me!" Raheem yelled as he teleported in and out of existence, punching Thaw from every angle.

Lincoln threw a punch in a random direction, hoping it would land. Raheem appeared right in front of him, and his fist connected powerfully with Raheem's chest. Raheem held the electrical charge in his body and focused his energy. He screamed as he focused the electrical current back at Lincoln, pushing him into the wall and losing his grip on the sword. Raheem teleported to the sword and disappeared with it in his hand.

"*Lincoln, I have the scroll,*" Thomas said through the earpiece. "*You need to read it as soon as this touches your hand. I'm running this over your location now!*"

"Be careful," Lincoln said. "Gorroff could be anywhere. Watch your six. Where was the scroll?"

"*It was in a stone coffin. My guess is that somebody put it there before Jesus was around or something,*" Thomas said.

Thomas ran over to the throne where the battle was still raging. Lincoln broke into a vicious sprint to retrieve the scroll before the

Spector materialized again. However, the Spector appeared in that moment just behind Thomas and grabbed him by the back. The Spector threw him to the ground in the opposite direction before turning to face Lincoln.

"You can't win, Thaw. I'm anywhere and everywhere, all at once. There is nothing I can't do." He ripped the scroll from Thomas's bloody hand. He held the scroll and cherished its power, but his moment of glory was shattered by a sudden, splitting migraine.

"Your attempt to read the scroll will be in vain, Raheem. You do not have the soul to read the scroll. Let Lincoln Thaw read it so that the world may be saved," Aura commanded.

Raheem ground his teeth and pointed the sword at Thomas. He twisted the blade, and a beam of energy blasted outward. Lincoln jumped in front of him and took the blast all by himself. His body shook with the energy he was absorbing. It eventually subsided thanks to the memory metal.

"You think you know how to save the world!" Raheem cried. Lincoln and Thomas were confused.

"As a matter of fact, we do," Thomas said.

"I wasn't talking to you," Raheem spat.

"We will save the world from you, Raheem, even if it's the last thing we do," Lincoln said.

"My name is the Golden Spector! Raheem Gorroff is dead!" Raheem screamed.

"You fulfilled your purpose to me, Raheem. Live your life and rid yourself of this pain. You have allowed the sins of your father to dictate your actions. In 556,876,445 other worlds, you overcame yourself to help Lincoln and Thomas with the world's problems. Please, let go so Thaw can read the scroll. Time grows short," Aura said.

"I don't care about the world!" Raheem yelled. "I don't care about the people in it, and I only care about seeing Lincoln dead at my hands!"

He began to charge at the pair of soldiers. Lincoln ran toward him at full speed. The two men clashed once more. Lincoln knocked

Excalibur out of Raheem's hands. Raheem was about to teleport away, but Lincoln activated the Particle Solidifier before he had the chance. Time ceased in suspended animation around the three men. Raheem's body was almost phased out of reality as if he was being erased from existence.

"The particles in your body are solidified in time right now. As long as the charge in this continues, you will not be going anywhere. So until then—" Lincoln continued.

He upper-cut Raheem in the face. He punched him as many times as he could before the timer on the Solidifier expired. Raheem's body was slowly dissipating, signifying that the effect was wearing off. Once the Solidifier depleted itself of all energy, he was gone, and the air was moving again.

"Where did he go?" Thomas yelled.

"Right here," Lincoln said as he turned his body and threw a punch at the open air.

To Thomas's shock, he saw Raheem being slammed back into existence. He hit the ground while Lincoln attempted to strangle him in a rage. Raheem felt the air being taken from him and choked. He began laughing like a maniac.

"How the hell did you see him before he showed up?" Thomas asked.

"He gets predictable," Lincoln said.

"You think you can kill me! I've only just begun with you!" the Spector said. He smacked Lincoln's fists out of the way and picked him up by the neck with one hand.

Thomas grabbed Excalibur and ran up to Raheem. He swung the blade at Raheem's arm. It sliced through, cutting it off entirely, and Lincoln fell back to the ground. The Spector screamed in agony as his body glowed brightly. However, the Spector's flesh materialized and overlapped itself, folding repeatedly until his arm regenerated and bones were once again covered with flesh and blood. His attention cut to the scroll that laid near them. He walked over and picked it up with ease.

"Remind me what you two idiots were here for again? Other than taking this magnificent scroll?" Raheem asked rhetorically.

"We wanted to come visit. You know, just see how your day was going," Thomas said sarcastically.

"This scroll is mine for the taking. I will destroy it and shall become unbeatable," Raheem said. "Every ally of America will succumb to my will. The world thinks its seen pain, but you've seen only a fraction of what can actually happen. When I'm done, democracy will be in the history books."

Raheem tried to open the scroll but couldn't. No matter how hard he tried, he simply couldn't open it. He struggled and pulled the paper open, but nothing budged.

"What's the matter? Why can't I open it?" he yelled.

"Because it's not your place, Gorroff," Lincoln said. "The verse said only someone who has the right intentions in their soul could read it. Yours is stained with vengeance and anger."

"No, no, no, this can't be! If I can't at least read this thing, then I'll have one hell of a time killing the likes of you both!" Raheem said, disappearing.

Lincoln knew exactly what to do. The Solidifier was charged once more and ready for combat. He activated it, and everything in the air froze. Raheem was now visible in the air, forced into a state of suspended animation once more.

Lincoln leaped into the air and snatched the scroll from the Spector's hands and landed with a thud. With ease, he unwrapped the ribbon and read the ancient poem within.

CHAPTER 17

Thou Excalibur holds truth and Purpose;
Its true power lies on the surface.
The prophecy tells of heroes and villains
With one mighty swing they are gone amongst the trillions.
Many worlds lay waste thanks to evil
There is no hope upon their retrieval.
This scroll was written and bewitched with purpose;
To save this world from eternal darkness.
Hold Excalibur firm and true,
It will surely attach itself to you.
Use it wisely never for evil;
This medieval blade is righteously lethal.
Place Excalibur to bask in the sunlight;
Be sure to gaze upon its celestial might.
When this scroll is complete in script and reading;
Take haste and go forth to your brand-new heading.
To you I ask: save this world;
Bring Balance to the stars and bestow freedom deserved.

Excalibur pulsated with light like a heartbeat. The wall crumbled and the floor shook from falling debris. Everywhere the three men looked, there was nothing but destruction. It timed out and shut down, allowing Raheem to get loose once more.

"Lincoln, I think we have a problem," Thomas said as Lincoln was suddenly struck in the face by Raheem.

Raheem walked over to him and kicked him numerous times before slamming his foot on his nose, breaking it through the memory metal. Lincoln could feel the *crack* and blood rushing out of his nose from the blow. Raheem grabbed him by the throat and began to slowly drain his life force. Slowly, Lincoln could feel his energy leaving his legs, arms, and mind. His skin began to shrivel up, and his eyes turned black.

"All this fighting gets you nowhere. I'll look into your eyes as you die slowly by my hand. I have seen the worst in people and let me say that you are nothing compared to them," Raheem stated.

Lincoln's face shriveled slowly as he aged. As fast as possible, he activated a flash grenade and braced himself. He closed his eyes and waited for the explosion.

"That's right, close your eyes and embrace—" Raheem said, just as a white explosion blinded him.

Lincoln's body was returning to life, and the wrinkles faded away as quickly as they had appeared. He stood tall and proud of his quick action. He bent down and picked up his mask, putting it back on his head and walking over to Excalibur. The walls around the temple were in ruin, allowing sunrays to invade and expose Excalibur to sunlight. He held the handle of the sword with both hands and thrust it high above his head, reaching toward the heavens. The sunlight hit the blade, and a light breeze picked up all around him. He closed his eyes for a minute to recall a quote from the scroll.

. . . be sure to gaze upon its celestial might, he thought.

The wind picked up, but Lincoln did not dare look away, in fear of what might come if he did. The clouds drifted away, and the sky grew blood red. The birds flew away in fear, and a bolt of lightning shot down from the sky, striking the sword. The Earth rumbled and vibrated. The terrain around them shook with the fierce winds. The lighting blended into numerous different colors. Red to blue, blue to yellow, yellow to orange, orange back to red. Finally, the lightning faded into a deep black sky. The sky then gave birth to a tornado of light, like it came from extraterrestrial origins. Lincoln held the sword firm and high over his head. He didn't look away from the supernatural forces presented before him.

"Here, I thought I've seen the worst," Thomas muttered, gazing upon the blackened sky. He noticed the Golden Spector staring at the events unfolding before him with concern.

"No, no, no, this isn't right!" he yelled. He pointed his arms at Lincoln to blast him away with his energy beams. "You have nothing to return to, Thaw!" Suddenly, Aura intruded into his subconscious for the last time.

"*Raheem Gorroff,*" Aura said. "*I cannot have you constantly attempting to overthrow my power by mindlessly taking what I've told you and changing my orders. I have observed every outcome of my own personal decision that I'm about to make, and every Earth that I do only proves that I have made the eloquent decision of making you a servant of the Multi-Precinct. I'm truly sorry that it's taken this much to teach you that you are wrong and your judgment is skewed by your vengeance.*"

"You don't know sh—" Raheem started until he felt his insides turning.

His stomach began to shift and convulse, and he vomited. He fell involuntarily to his knees as his golden skin shriveled and condensed and deformed to the point where his bones protruded slightly. His now gaunt face changed to a deep grey. Some of his teeth chipped and fell away. His limbs also changed color with the rest of his body. His eyes that once glowed blood red were now back to their mortal brown, but his pupils continued to dilate until his eyes were completely black. His jawbone snapped, and it dangled from only one side of his face. He was a true horror, a true monster.

"Jesus, mother—" Thomas whispered.

A deformed and hollow version of what used to be the Golden Spector stood before them. The creature roared as a bolt of lightning erupted from Excalibur, hitting the beast. In a flash, the elongated creature was zapped out of existence without a trace.

Thomas turned to Lincoln, who still held the sword aloft. The lightning swarmed around him, engulfing the sky. It changed colors throughout the entire color spectrum. The ground rumbled and shook, and the sword floated out of Lincoln's grasp.

Lincoln and Thomas looked up in amazement as a black hole formed in the sky above them. The sword floated higher into the endless black void. The pair watched in awe as the weapon opened a gateway to another world.

Aura meditated and focused on the energy that was beaming and pulsating from Earth. She slowly opened her eyes and whispered a few words that would correct the interdimensional abnormality that had been unbalanced for thousands of years.

"Excalibur almighty, be free from this place. Return to your dimension with great haste," she said. Just then, the sword began to glow once more.

"If we die from this, I'm gonna seriously miss my future welfare checks," Thomas said. "What's it doing?"

The sword emitted such a powerful pulse that it rocked into the core of the black hole. Seconds after, the black hole dissipated. The sun broke through the black clouds, emitting rays of light. Thomas and Lincoln kept their eyes on the sky as Excalibur disappeared with the singularity.

"Well, where did it go?" Thomas asked.

"I don't know. Probably back to wherever it came from," Lincoln replied.

"So we spent all that time for it to up and leave?" Thomas shouted.

"No, we did our jobs, and that's the best we could've done. It's over now. What happened to the Spector?"

"Did you not see him? He . . . he's gone. That's all I know," Thomas said. He shivered, remembering the grotesque sight.

"When you're holding a sword in the air with the sky swirling around you like the end of the world, you don't normally look anywhere else. Maybe all that power finally killed him for good."

"Maybe, but he didn't look dead in the slightest. He looked undead."

"Let's get the hell out of here before someone comes up here to find out what happened."

"Too late," Lincoln said as he pointed to the ground at the base of the mountain. Far below, the men and women of the local village were flocking over to the area in curiosity.

"It's best if we get out of here while we still can. I don't want to draw too much attention," Lincoln said.

"Consider it done," Thomas said as he tapped the Bluetooth earpiece. "Thomas to Adam, we're ready for departure," he said over the intercom.

There was a long pause before finally the pair were engulfed in a green flash and vanished from the rocky battlefield. When the pair re-entered the compound, they were greeted with a horrible sight. Adam's main lab was torn to shreds. Tables were flipped over and broken, computer monitors were smashed on the ground, the walls were caved in and beaten, and traces of blood stained the plain white walls.

"Raheem said we would have nothing to come home to," Lincoln said. "Where's Adam? Look for him!"

"*Thermal Detection Mode initiated, human recovery scanning in progress,*" said the electronic voice inside Lincoln's mask.

His vision turned blue as his surroundings began changing colors. If he found Adam, he would know before Thomas due to his advantage. Ironically, no such technology was needed when they heard a faint cry for help. The pair rushed toward the hallway, where they found Adam face down on the ground. His clothes were shredded and bloody, and the ground was blood-stained. His bruised hand rested on the retrieval button.

"He's still alive, thank God," Thomas said while checking his pulse.

"We need to get him to a hospital now," Lincoln said. "Is there anyone else in the building?"

"Scanning for thermal heat signatures in the building," the technological voice inside Lincoln's suit said. Within a few seconds, it spoke again. *"No heat signatures identified. Facility clear of any and all life."*

Lincoln scooped up Adam and followed Thomas out to the nearest exit. The Spector had really destroyed the place. It was an awful sight. It was as if the Spector had wanted to recreate the BULL incident all over again.

★ ★ ★

"Sentara Norfolk General Hospital located. Proceed straight and take the first left immediately," the voice commanded.

In the distance, he could see a bright sign that read "Sentara." He was filled with hope, and his heart raced. The building grew closer with each passing second.

"Hang on, buddy," Lincoln said.

Finally, they arrived at the emergency room. He placed Adam on the bed and started powering on the machines to revitalize him. He was used to the life-support machines from his time in the military. He activated the mini-electrodes on his hands and lowered the intensity of the electrical charge. Then without a second's thought, he placed his fist on Adam's chest and shocked Adam just enough to see his body convulse from the electrical current. There was no response from him. He tried again, but there was still nothing. Finally, he increased the intensity and slammed his fist on him. Adam gasped for air and vomited blood. Two doctors rushed in the room. "This man needs immediate assistance and reconfiguration on his lungs," one of the doctors commanded. Blood was erupting from Adam's mouth while he struggled for air.

"Any doctors who are not currently assisting anyone, I have a man who's in pretty bad shape here and I need equipment ASAP!" Thaw heard another doctor shout as he slipped silently out the window.

Lincoln jumped down and landed on the rooftop below. He walked over to view the Sentara Hospital from afar so he was not visible. The sounds of the city below were all he heard.

Thaw watched the night city and gazed upon its neon beauty once more to calm down from all the madness. As he watched, rain poured down and overtook everything around him. Even through the suit, he could feel the bitterly cold rain. He lowered his head and closed his eyes to recall everything he had been through. He pulled off his mask to be exposed to the elements. He felt his hair grow wet as droplets trickled down his neck. He took deep breaths and looked up to the stormy sky, wondering if Adam was going to pull through.

A large and lengthy creature stood in a dark, decrepit forest. As it hunched over, its back cracked and snapped. With each muscle movement, its joints popped and became even more disfigured. With each step that the creature took, it growled and snarled at the darkness surrounding it. The Spector was no longer human, but an unholy masterpiece constructed by the watcher of worlds. The very essence of life itself served no purpose in this place. Rather, it was silent with no hope. This place, this alternate version of Earth, was a conception no human would desire to experience. The monstrosity moved in agony, with each step more painful than the last. The being spotted a clearing and walked to it. Its skull was just barely visible in the shadows, with webs protruding outward from his decaying flesh. The crimson octagon that once fueled the Spector's power was now a desolate, empty black shell devoid of life.

It paced slowly through a ghost-like fog and peered upward to the sky. The night above held no stars, no moon, and no clouds. In a fit of rage, the beast raised its long and lengthy arms to the heavens and belted out a roar of anguish and turmoil. Banished by the Aura, this creature craved only flesh and blood. Without recollection of any previous existence, it began its carnivorous hunt.

CHAPTER 18

"SIGHTINGS OF MYSTERIOUS LIGHTS IN the sky over rural Britain were present yesterday, causing many to wonder what caused this strange phenomenon," said the anchorman. *"Many of the townspeople who were in the neighboring villages near the mountain where it happened claimed to have seen an array of multicolored lightning illuminating the sky. Let's hear what one of the townspeople has to say about the matter."*

"It was as if God opened a portal from heaven himself," said a local woman onscreen. *"I don't know what could've possibly done that, but in all my sixty years of living here, I've never seen anything like that. It was almost like some kind of storm, but no storm I've ever seen could have changed colors like that. I'm just happy it's over."*

"Britain has a long history of strange, religious events that have occurred over thousands of years," said the anchorman, returning to the screen once more. *"But this is the only one to be recorded in modern history. The world's leading scientists are now investigating and trying to discover exactly what phenomena could have caused*

these lights in the sky to appear. The government has assembled all the brightest minds in the nation to assist in the investigation."

The screen then switched to an aerial view of the mountaintop littered with investigators with white gloves taking pictures of the temple's remains. Helicopters circled everywhere, lowering scientists to join in on the investigation. Weather balloons were being deployed into the sky above, along with numerous drones, to scope out the area even further. The screen panned back to the anchor once more.

"The nations of the world are still in awe of the mysterious events that transpired on the top of the mountain," said the anchorman. *"In other news, the globally known terrorist, Raheem Gorroff, was declared missing by the United Nations this morning. The authorities believe that he may be in hiding to rebuild the Souls of Death headquarters in response to his father's death declared earlier this month. This is George O'Brian reporting live."*

Veronica turned off the TV and set the remote on the table next to Ben's bed. His face was badly bruised, and his left eye was swollen shut. He still couldn't feel his legs. He only just woke up an hour ago, and he was still recuperating.

"What . . . happened?" he asked, looking over to Veronica. She leaned in close and moved her fingertips through his hair to calm him down.

"The Golden Spector is dead," she whispered. "We won."

A feeling of pure relief washed over him as he heard it.

"Lincoln? Thomas? The kids?" His heart monitor beeped faster.

Veronica put her hands on his chest to calm him down. "They're all fine. I just heard from Lincoln. He and Thomas are on their way over."

He calmed down and rested his head back against the pillow. A tall doctor walked in with a white coat and a clipboard.

"Mr. Frost, it's a relief that you're finally awake," the doctor said.

"Although I've been better," he said. "A whole lot better. What happened?" He noticed that Veronica's smile was almost plastered on. He knew something was off. He was growing scared without answers.

"What did you guys do to me? Did you put another steel plate in my back?" he asked, only half serious. A long pause followed. Veronica looked away and held his shoulder.

"Mr. Frost, your spine was severed in three different spots, causing extreme muscular and bone damage. We had to take extensive action to save you. However, your legs were permanently affected by this and—"

"Just tell me what you guys did!" he interrupted irritably. Veronica turned back to him very gently.

"Honey, you're paralyzed from the waist down. They tried every option, but nothing looked promising. Your body was so battered that they didn't know if you were gonna pull through, with or without your legs."

This wasn't supposed to happen, he thought.

He'd had taken his share of shrapnel, but the gunfire and explosions in Iraq had never left him in such bad condition. He closed his eyes in anguish.

"Every one of your cervical vertebrae down has been crushed or cracked in some way. I'm so terribly sorry. We were able to implant metal rods to better align your back," she said with sadness.

Veronica looked at Ben with concern. She held his hand in support.

"What . . . kind of life will I live?" Ben asked.

"We've contacted Roland Industries to see if they would have any mechanical advancements to help you walk, but they rejected our request for more suitable applicants."

"What the hell do they mean that I'm not a suitable applicant? If they need proof, I can wheel myself in there and show them I can't walk!"

Veronica tried to calm him down and kissed him on the cheek. He took a few deep breaths and laid his head on the pillow once more.

"Was it the severity of his condition that kept them from approving his case?" she asked.

"The machine they are testing to help wounded soldiers move

around again needs to be surgically implanted, and your case is so severe that the surgery alone will very likely kill you."

"I'm so sorry. We tried everything that we could. I hope you understand," the doctor said.

A long pause echoed after she spoke. All that could be heard was the ceiling fan spinning above. In a mixture of anger, sadness, dread, and heartache, Ben just nodded his head.

"I understand, doctor," he said. "Thanks for everything." She nodded her head and slowly walked out of the room.

"What are the kids gonna think of their crippled dad?" he asked.

"They will love and care about you just like they always have," Veronica said.

"I thought I was gonna run with them while they rode a bike without training wheels for the first time. I thought I was gonna walk with you on a beach while watching the sunset."

"We can still do all those things. I'm going to help you through sickness and health, remember?"

"How are we gonna raise the kids?" he asked.

"We'll do it together. Nothing on this planet will prevent you from living your life. The important thing is that you're here. Even if you're in a wheelchair, you're still my husband, and I will always love you for who you are. We will always stick together through thick and thin. Benjamin Frost, look at me," she said.

He kept his head pointed to the bedsheets. She lightly tapped her fingertip with his chin and pushed his face upward to meet hers.

"You're alive. That's a reward in its own right. You, Lincoln, and Thomas have gone through so much in your lives, and this does not define who you are. Your story is not over: there's another page that needs to be turned. Especially when I'm still around, okay?"

Ben rested his head on her shoulder and continued to sob loudly.

"I love you so much," he blurted.

Veronica wrapped her arms around him and hugged him close. "I love you, too."

★ ★ ★

Lincoln and Thomas were back in the hangar below ground in Norfolk. The pair rested in the ruined remains of what used to be Adam's office. The light fixtures hanging above were flickering as they sat in silence, trying to take in everything. Their faces were a mixture of happiness and shock.

"So we graduated ourselves from military asshats to superheroes, huh?" asked Thomas. "I like that. Puts a good description on our resume."

"We don't tell anybody about this," Lincoln said. "If our secret were to get out, then our families and friends would be in extreme danger. We can't afford something like that to happen."

"So we go incognito for the rest of our lives about this?" Thomas asked.

"We have to. But hey, you kicked ass back there *and* you did the best you could," Lincoln said. "You're just lucky that the sword healed you as fast as it did or else you would've been six feet under."

"Have you contacted Ben or Veronica?" Thomas asked.

"Yeah, I told Veronica we'd be over as soon as we could. I can only imagine how they are right now. Let's get these things off of us and head over there," Lincoln replied.

Thomas hesitantly put his suit inside a transparent suitcase with the Roland Industries logo on the front. Lincoln put his suit back on the mannequin and silently closed the glass door to protect it. Thomas walked up behind him, crossing his arms.

"You're not gonna keep it?" Thomas asked. "I sure would."

"I can't keep this, Thomas. As much as I would love to, it's not my place. Adam worked so hard to make this suit to save the world. The least I can do is give him something in return. Too many people in this world are tainted with greed and hunger for power. But I'm not. I'm gonna leave him with a gift for helping us."

With a single hiss, the case was locked and sealed. Lincoln backed away from the glass case and crossed his arms. The pair just stared at the glass case for one final time before leaving.

"You think you're ever going to wear it again?" Thomas asked.

"Never again," Lincoln stated. "I'm an American sniper who'll protect his country no matter the cost. Not a superhero who has the weight of the world on his shoulders."

Deep down, he loved every second of wearing the mighty suit, as it made him feel in control of every possible situation. For years, he was so used to being behind a rifle that the feeling of hand-to-hand combat faded. He only used tactical situations as a last resort, but every time he threw a punch in the suit, he felt like he was truly invincible.

As he gazed upon the suit's black fabric, he had a revelation: power was a great tool to have and to hold most dear, but power came at a great cost. The suit's abilities were intoxicating and blinded him to the essence of a true hero: knowing one's true power and limitations in order to stay content with one's own life.

"What if someone or something like the Spector rises again? What then?" Thomas asked.

"Adam will get someone else for the job, I know it, but until we see this thing again—" Lincoln shut off the lights.

He turned to walk away, and they exited the badly damaged room. Thomas stood in the dimly lit hallway waiting for him to close the door. Lincoln stopped and stood looking over his shoulder to glance at the suit one final time.

"Let's hope the world stays safe for now," he said as he locked the door.

Thomas called Veronica again, asking her what room Ben was in. She explained that they were relocated to the Naval Medical Center in Portsmouth, Virginia. Ben's room was 1226 on the fifth floor. She then asked if she could speak to Lincoln, and Thomas handed him the phone.

"Told you we'd make it out okay, and you didn't believe me," Lincoln joked.

"Jesus, Lincoln," she said. *"It's on the news now."*

"What are they saying?" he asked.

"They're mostly just speculating what happened up on that mountain," she said.

"Thank God," he replied. "The last thing I want is the whole world looking at me like the president of the US. Oh, and Raheem's gone if you were wondering."

"Good riddance. What happened to him?" she asked.

"You wouldn't believe us if we told you," Lincoln said. "He's gone now, and that's all that matters. We'll tell ya about it once we get there."

The pair made their way to the Naval Medical Center. Patients were lined up in the hallways. One could barely walk, and others were simply trying to find space to rest. Finally, they found the Frost family. Once they entered, the kids raced to them and embraced their legs. For the first time since all the madness, Lincoln and Thomas smiled.

"How you doing, little guys?" Thomas said, picking up Theia. She giggled. Lincoln hugged Zachary and noticed Ben staring at them with a smile.

"About time we saw each other again," Ben said quietly. Lincoln rose and walked over to his bed.

"I was starting to get a little worried about you, man," he said. "Still alive, I see."

"Well, I think my walking days are done," Ben said. "That Charlie Roland is a no-good punk. He could have let me have his new walking prototype they just developed, but apparently my case is 'too risky.'" Veronica shot him a glare, and he continued. "However, I'm glad that I'm still alive. That's what matters."

"It's a damn good thing, too," said Lincoln. "The world's safe as well. You know, I never in a million years thought that I'd say that."

"By the way, I caught some radio chatter that they were going to rebuild BULL," Thomas said. "But they're going to call it something else."

"As long as they can build stuff that saves the world from threats like Gorroff, I'm down," Lincoln said. "Are they still owned by Roland?"

"You bet they are," Thomas replied.

"Would've been nice if they were privately owned, but I'm just thinking out loud," Lincoln responded.

"So what exactly happened on that mountain?" Ben asked.

"Yeah, what do you remember?" Veronica chimed in.

"I know it sounds like I dropped acid when I say it, but this voice—of the sword, I guess—spoke through the halls of the temple we were in," Lincoln said. "All I really remember was that it said something about speaking 'the words that free the text, let the world be free . . . ' Or something like that."

"Words that free the text? What did it mean by free the text?" Ben asked.

"If it meant 'free the text,' then it obviously means that something was holding that power captive for who knows how long," Veronica spoke up.

"Let's not talk ridiculous stuff like that. Come on. There can't be some huge conspiracy going on here," Thomas said.

"Why not? If my daughter was sucked into a portal and the legend of Excalibur was true, your run-in with a being that claimed to be a world-watcher and the existence of actual superpowers, then nothing is impossible," Lincoln said.

"What happened to the sword, then?" Veronica asked. Thomas smiled.

"It disappeared after the black hole opened over the mountain," Lincoln said.

"So, wait, the sword chose you to restore balance," Thomas remarked. "So, by legend, that technically makes you the king of England." He laughed.

"I guess . . . you're right . . . for once." Lincoln chuckled.

"Lincoln, Thomas is right! Whoever's worthy of Excalibur is the rightful king. Are you gonna live there now?" Ben teased.

"Hell no, I'm not moving anywhere; I'm happy where I am. Even if I am the unofficial king of Britain. Besides, it'll look good on my resume."

"Ya know, you can use that for any leverage for future fights," Veronica said.

"Let's hope I never have to," Lincoln said.

Thomas went back home to Northern Virginia along with the Frost family, visiting Ben every day until he got better. Lincoln went back to his rural house in Virginia Beach. The dirty gravel road was welcoming him. The wind was whipping inside the truck through the windows, filled with the scent of pollen and distant flowers.

He parked the truck inside the garage.

From the corner of his eye, he spotted something covered with a blue tarp. It was a car indeed, but who had the courage to break into his garage and put a car in it? A little note was left on the hood of the mystery car that read: *"Found it in the junkyard and thought of you."*

It was from Adam. He grabbed the tarp anxiously and yanked it, exposing a breathtaking sight. Before him was a faded black two-door 1957 Cadillac Coup Deville. It had a missing headlight along with a rusted chrome grill. He opened the door, and the latch came loose, causing the door to disconnect and fall to the floor. He laughed a little at the situation. He looked inside and noticed that the interior was ripped to pieces.

He smiled to himself and knew he had to thank Adam later. It was no coincidence that this car was black and matched his suit.

He walked outside over to the sliding door and pulled it down, taking the small note with him.

Dear Lincoln,

You've shown me what it's like to fully trust someone with "my" property. Especially when it comes to saving the world. I never would've imagined my inventions would end up saving so much, and I thank you for that. I admire that you gave the suit back to me, but I want to give you something back you earned. Keep this; it may be a little beat up, but it's nothing you can't handle. Thank you for saving me and everyone else. Rest easy, and I wish you luck on your future endeavors.

Adam X. Braxton

He put the note down. The only sound he heard was the wind whistling through the windows along with the breeze pushing against the corn stalks. He got up and walked to the island in the middle of the kitchen and pulled out the journal he wrote in when he was in the service.

July 3, 2011,

It's amazing just what a few days can do to anyone with the power to save lives on a daily basis. The Gorroffs are not a threat anymore. One is missing and the other is apparently "undead," at least according to Thomas. I couldn't care less where they are as long as they won't inflict pain on innocent people. For now, taking it easy will be my main priority. Saving the world is science fiction for most, but a slight reality for few. I don't know what the future holds, but one thing is certain for me. Out of all the craziness of seeing supernatural events unfold in front of me, I have realized that nothing is truly impossible. I can only say that I have to keep moving forward and protect the ones that I love. Now I see and understand that I am a hero to most but savior to few. It's a strange feeling that you saved more than a billion lives and no one knows who you are.

I really wish that my baby girl can see what I've done so that she would have grown up in a world free of injustice and magical bullshit, but we all know that the world I'm referencing doesn't exist. I wish I could tuck her in bed at night and tell her all those classic bedtime stories, watch as her imagination raced, and protect her as she closed her eyes to dream away. I miss those nights, but we all have to move on. Wherever she is, I know that she's smiling and cheering me on. Until the next journal entry, I'll update my new persona as the one and only "Marksman," such a catchy ring to it.

Suddenly, the breeze picked up, interrupting his writing. He remembered that he forgot to close the garage. He ran outside to do so before everything got soaked. The wind started to pound the window. The sky above started to churn with dark clouds. Thunder cracked the silence of the once-serene environment. Everything was being tossed around by hurricane-level winds. Nothing made sense. The forecast called for clear skies and warm temperatures. Now it was thunderstorms and cool air. Virginia weather was unpredictable, sure, but this was different. Something wasn't right.

Quickly, he ran to the shed to take down anything outside that would potentially fly away, when he was halted by a clashing bolt of lightning that struck right in front of him. Never in his life had his ears been so rocked. The thunder that followed was unnaturally loud, and he fell to the ground, covering his ears in pain. All he could hear was ringing for a solid two minutes. The wind increased, but he attempted to get up and make a break for the house when he was halted again by the sight of twirling light appear in front of him. It circled and moved around repeatedly until it created one circular beam. Lincoln watched the supernatural event unfold before him in horror. Nothing but black could be seen inside the portal until a bright flash of gold emanated from the circular mystery. He heard a voice cry out to him. A child's voice.

"Daddy! Dad, can you hear me? You have to save me! I love you so much! I don't have much time before—" The voice was suddenly cut off as the portal was dispersed by another bolt of lightning from above. All was calm now, and the lighting was chased immediately by thunder. Rain poured down in torrents as Lincoln lay motionless on the grass. His blood ran cold in realization.

" . . . Patty," he whispered.

ACKNOWLEDGMENTS

IN WRITING THIS BOOK, I'VE learned so much about this art form. I had no idea of the amount of collaboration this would take. In this process, I've learned that the artistic field is its own beast. It takes precision, a clear mind, perseverance, and above all, patience. Growing up, I never wanted to be an author or write a book for fun. To me, that's what nerds did. Life's ironic, isn't it?

When I was nine years old, I wrote a small *Spider-Man* comic that had him fight all his villains on a poorly drawn piece of paper. I guess that was the beginning. When I was a sophomore in high school, I wrote a small novelette in which I gave all my friends superpowers and put them in real situations. Some people thought it was great, and some thought it was illiterate garbage. I even misspelled the damned title. But I knew then that my calling was to tell a good damn story.

After I graduated from high school, I attended Tidewater Community College, or TCC, in the fall of 2017, and began my studies there for an associates in the general studies. I had an idea of where I wanted to go after TCC, but my vision wasn't totally clear. However, I had a new inspiration after my Film Appreciation class showed us the 2014 film *American Sniper*. That film resonated with me in a way that previous war films did not. Something about the internal struggle of Chris Kyle and his endless pursuit of justice made me realize that real superheroes are indeed among us. Also, how cool would it be if it had a science fiction twist?

Little did I know that question would catapult me in writing this novel. From this process, I have learned the virtues of character development, story arcs, and the basic formula for writing a story people give a damn about.

There are people that I'd like to formally give thanks to and acknowledge to the support of this book reaching print. First of all, I have to thank my mother and father. Without their loving support of reaching this gargantuan milestone in my life, this would've been so much harder. I'm beyond blessed to still have you in my journey. I'd like to thank my amazing artist, photographer, and editor, Rachel Vredenburg. I owe you a ton of gratitude and thanks. No one has helped me bring a craft across the finish line as you did. Without your support and precious time, this would not have been completed in such a timely fashion.

I'd like to thank the TCC event coordinator Mrs. Sara Hair for supporting me for the three years I was enrolled. Thank you for listening to me and motivating me. I made that leap of faith you encouraged, and I don't regret it at all. I had one economics and personal finance teacher from my high school years that always believed in me. Thank you, Mr. David Thaw, for refusing to let me quit when I was on the verge of giving up on myself.

A much-appreciated thanks is also owed to Pastor Thomas Ondrea. No one else I knew when I was younger had the compassion and motivational skills you did, and I owe you big time for that one. There are many more positive attributes that I'd list, but I have to acknowledge one more person that helped in this project.

Grandma, I wish you were still around to read this, but look! I did it! I finished it as I promised I would! Thank you for taking an interest in my pursuit to live my life to the fullest. You watched me grow along with my cousins and siblings, and I thank you for always being there for someone to talk to and take advice from. I couldn't have asked for a better grandmother. You were right as well: it is a good life.

CONCEPTUAL DESIGNS

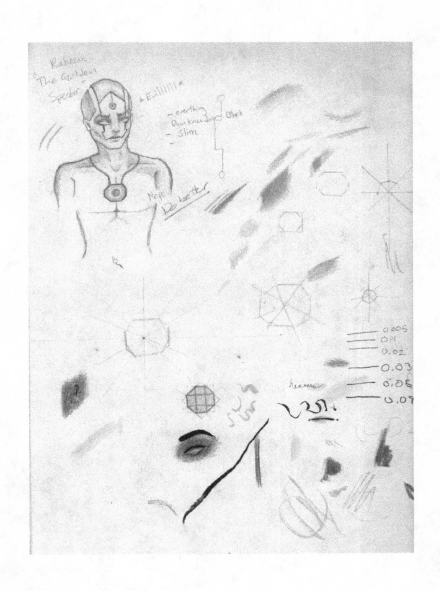

• Aura

- golden square
- Mostly blue (hair)
- no pupils, yellow eyes
- whites of eyes + blue
- galaxy/nebula + everything
- goddess like, flirty
- nebulas

— vary [illegible]
(Deadon[?]
gree[?]

Sketchbook size

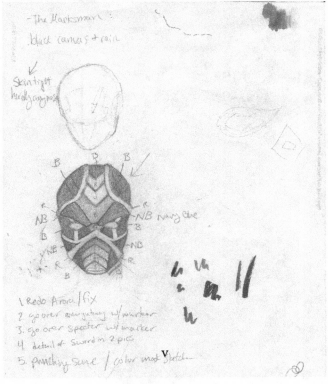

- The Marksman:
black canvas + rain

Skin tight
hard gay pas

B   B   B

R   R
NB   NB navy blue
B   B
NB   NB
R   R
B   B

1 Redo Arrow / fix
2 go over everything w/ marker
3. go over specter w/ marker
4 detail of sword in 2 pics
5. punching scene / color mock Sketch

- long fingers like small knife ⊙
- shriveled skin
- visible bones (slightly)
- grey face
- shaked teeth
- completly black eyes
- jaw snapped

face 3/4

Arms profile